Bound By Blood

Rogues of Magic Book 1

Tiffany Shand

DEDICATION

For my mum, Karen.

PROLOGUE

Ann Valeran crouched low in the bushes as she stared at the small stone building. It was round in shape and made of crumbling grey stone. A remnant from before the dark times, before all the world of Erthea had changed.

Branches snagged at her long cloak. Its black colour helped her blend in with her surroundings, and she pulled its long length over her knees.

You sure this is the right place? she asked in thought, then turned to stare at Edward Rohn, her best friend.

He knelt beside her, unmoving. *This is where the message said the witness wanted to meet us.*

How do we even know this so-called witness is legitimate? Her eyes narrowed at him. *It's been five years. It seems strange someone would come forward after all this time.*

Isn't it worth finding out? Ed's dark brown eyes seemed almost black in the darkness.

Ann sighed, pushing her long, wavy blonde hair off her face to tuck it underneath her hood. This was it. The chance she'd been waiting over five years for. A chance to prove to all five lands that she hadn't murdered her family.

How did the witness even know where to find us? she asked, sitting back on the cold, hard earth.

Above, the night sky hung like a heavy blanket of darkness, without a cloud or glittering star in sight. It made it much easier for Ann and Ed to stay concealed without using magic. Magic would make it easier for Gliss or any other potential enemies to find them.

Ann could see easily in the near blackness. As a druid, she used her fire element to make everything seem lighter and enhance her vision.

She knew as one of the Black Guard, Ed saw clearly too. It was strange how the magic of her father's old guard had survived after all this time.

Ed touched her shoulder. *Don't you want the chance to prove your innocence?* In the low light, she made out his short brown hair, golden brown eyes, and chiselled face.

His touch felt comforting, but Ann bit her lip. She hated being hunted by Orla's forces, not to mention all the others who sought to profit from the price on her head. She didn't know how high the price had grown but had heard it was almost ten thousand coins now. Enough to make someone comfortable for the rest of their life.

Yes, Ann said. *But it won't bring my family back or restore my father's lands to me.*

Darius Valeran had been the archdruid of Caselhelm on the night of the revolution. He had not just controlled Caselhelm, but parts of the other territories as well. Under his rule, the lands had been at peace for the first time in ten thousand years. The Realm War began that night at the hands of the Fomorian demon Orla, when Ann's parents, Darius and Deanna, had been murdered. After the latest realm war, peace was a distant memory. Orla had won control over most of Caselhelm and placed a bounty on Ann's head.

A witness had reached out to one of Ann's contacts in the resistance, claiming to be one of Orla's associates. She said she would approach the council—a small governing body who oversaw the rule of the five lands—to tell them the truth about what happened to Ann's parents.

Ed gave her hand a comforting squeeze as she rose.

Ann took a deep breath. *Let's get this over with. I want to get back to the warehouse before Xander wakes up.* She was glad she hadn't brought her brother along with them. At least then he'd be safe if this turned out to be a trap.

Ann stayed alert as she scanned the area. She searched for potential threats but sensed no other presences nearby.

She and Ed moved over to the building, which only had one outer door. That made Ann more uneasy; she liked having more than one escape route when she went somewhere unknown. *Do you sense anyone inside?* she asked.

He shook his head. *No one.*

Let's make this quick. The familiar weight of her knives at her back felt comforting.

Ed pulled the wooden door open. It gave a groan of protest as he did so. Ann half expected it to fall off its hinges given the age of the building.

Ann paused, scanning the building with her mind. She used the earth lines, feeling the hum of power, but nothing suggested the presence of another living being nearby. Earth lines were veins of natural power that run through Earth itself. Some called them the world's lifeblood.

"Maybe the witness isn't here yet," Ed whispered, touching the hilt of the sword at his back.

"I don't like this," Ann remarked. "We should have picked a neutral location, somewhere in the other lands, not Caselhelm."

She glanced around the empty passageway, then touched the stone, which groaned and mumbled. Stone magic was rare among the druids, but her power could tap into almost all of the elements.

Ann closed her eyes, listening. This place had been a bunker. She heard people screaming and the sound of running footsteps as the stones showed her what had happened here.

Nice place to meet someone who claims they can prove I'm not a murderer.

Ann let go of the stone, and the murmurs faded. "What do we know about the witness? You haven't told me anything about them."

"Sage didn't tell me much." Ed shrugged and moved ahead of her, keeping a close eye out for potential threats.

"When does she ever?" She hated talking to the other druid at the best of times. Ann had been suspicious when Sage contacted Ed in thought with the news about the witness.

"She seemed to trust this person."

"This person who wouldn't even give us their name." Ann grimaced as she walked face-first into some spider-webs. She brushed them off with the back of her hand. "I like to know the details. Next time, *I'll* talk to Sage."

Ed chuckled. "Careful, there might still be spiders around here."

She scowled at him. "Don't mention spiders around me. They are almost as bad as Sage."

"You hate talking to her, even though she's your aunt."

"She is *not* my aunt. She's my aunt's lover, there's a difference." Ann rounded a corner, following a passageway that led into a larger room. Ancient debris and dirt littered the stone floor. Withered black leaves crunched under her feet as she walked in. No one here, and there was no other entrance, so they'd have had to come in the same way she and Ed did.

"Are you sure Sage didn't tell you anything else?" Ann prompted.

Ed pulled out his sword, the blade catching the light as Ann lit a crystal torch on the wall that filled the room with an orange glow. Shadows danced across the stone floor.

"Stop being so worried. That's my job." Ed grinned.

"Not anymore. You haven't been my bodyguard in over five years. You're my partner."

"I've always been your partner. Always and forever, remember?"

Ann smiled at the promise they'd made to each other as kids. Always and forever best friends.

She sighed, using the lines to tell the time. Just past midnight, when their witness had said she'd be there.

"Try to keep an open mind," Ed said. "What if this person truly wants to help?"

Ann didn't trust anyone, not after everything she'd been through. The only two people she did trust with her life were Ed and Xander.

A lack of faith in others had kept her alive. She didn't dare hope this person would help.

"Let's be ready to make a quick exit. Stay close to me so I can transport us out as quickly as possible."

"Let's see what they have to say first."

Ann frowned. "You keep defending them. What aren't you telling me?" She put her hands on her hips. "Edward Rohn, you've never been able to lie to me. Tell me what you're hiding."

"Nothing." Ed shook his head. "I'm not…" He gritted his teeth. "I just want you to talk to her."

"*Her?*" Ann's eyes narrowed to slits. "You do know who's coming." She pulled out one of her knives as the once smooth earth lines became jagged beneath her feet, warning her of another presence. *Someone's here.*

Orla? No, Edward wouldn't set up a meeting with the demon bitch who'd helped murder her parents and had killed or enslaved thousands of Magickind in her tyrannical rule.

"Who's coming?" she hissed.

He said nothing and shook his head again.

A woman with long raven hair past her shoulders walked in. Her

8

skin was pale, her eyes so dark they looked almost like obsidian. She wore a red version of the leather bodysuit all Gliss wore. It covered her from neck to toe.

It took Ann a second to place the woman's face as that of Ceara Mason, once a close friend, now a traitor who'd helped destroy her family.

Ed, you can't be serious, Ann growled.

Ann, please just listen to what she has to say, Ed replied.

Heat flared between her fingers as her fire magic burned to life.

Ceara studied them and smiled her perfect smile. Ceara had always been a dark beauty, which had drawn Ann's brothers to her.

Ann, with her own pale skin, long blonde hair, and pale blue eyes, looked slight compared to Ceara's darkness. Ed and Ceara were both taller than her.

"Rhiannon, it's been a long time." Ceara smirked. "I hear they're calling you the rogue archdruid now."

"What do you want, Ceara?" Ann folded her arms. Any hope of this witness being genuine had long faded. Oh, Ceara had been there. Only she'd been on the enemy's side. She knew this was a setup. Still, she couldn't believe Edward had agreed to go along with it.

"I expected a warmer welcome. I mean, we haven't seen—"

"Why are you here?" Ann snapped. "Don't give me some crap about wanting to turn against Orla. We both know where your loyalties lie."

Ceara's smile faded. "That *is* why I'm here. Spirits, I thought you'd be tired of life as a fugitive."

"What makes you think I'd ever accept your help?" The fire between her fingers blazed harsh and hot. Her magic wanted out, wanted to kill this traitorous bitch.

"Say what you want to say, Ceara." Ed took Ann's hand. The flames licked his skin but snuffed out as he squeezed her hand. Her fire wouldn't harm him; he'd always been immune to it.

"Wolfy, it's been a long time. I—"

Ed gave Ceara a hard look. "You stopped being my foster sister a long time ago. You don't get to call me that."

Ceara sighed. "I'm here because I made a mistake the night I helped Orla and Urien. I didn't kill either of your parents, Ann. If you don't believe anything else I say, believe that. Listen, I'm one of the few people who can prove you didn't kill your parents," Ceara snapped.

"You really expect me to believe you want to help?" Ann scoffed. "Why would you do that?"

"Because I'm tired of living under Orla's rule. She's…it's not important," Ceara replied. "Don't you want to come out of hiding, Rhiannon?"

Ann winced at Ceara's continued use of her full name. Rhiannon Valeran had died along with her parents. Along with her life as the archdruid's daughter. It wasn't who or what she was any more.

"I'd rather hide than be ruled by Orla."

"That's why I'm here. Since she took over, magic is outlawed in Caselhelm, and those who have it are kept under strict control. Even among the Gliss," Ceara said. "Orla has to be stopped, and you're the only one who can do it. I'll come with you and tell the council what really happened."

Ann shook her head, knowing Ceara wouldn't help her. This was ridiculous. Even as a child, selflessness had never been her strong suit. There had to be some other motivation. Anyway, on the slim chance she did want to help, there was no guarantee the council would believe her.

"If we buy this, what do you get out of it?" Ed prompted.

"Why can't you believe I just want to help?" Ceara demanded.

"Because you're a Gliss who helped Orla destroy everything my father worked for," Ann snapped.

"I've made mistakes, but aren't you willing to take the risk to stop Orla?"

Ann laughed. "You expect us to believe you want to turn on her. Do you take us for idiots?"

"Aren't you and your resistance friends trying to do just that?" Ceara arched an eyebrow. "I've heard the rumours. I know how you help them flee Orla's clutches."

Ann gritted her teeth. They weren't here to discuss the resistance. The last thing she needed was Ceara finding out anything about them. She only hoped Sage hadn't divulged any details about them to Ceara.

"If you truly want us to trust you, you're going to have to prove it," Ed challenged.

"I came here, didn't I?" Ceara threw up her hands in surrender. "You have no idea what Orla would do if she found out I came to see you."

Ed, let's just get out of here, Ann said. *I can't do this. We're wasting our time. Let's get back to Xander. She'll never help us. She's just leading us into a trap.*

Ceara reached into a pocket of her bodice. "I did bring something to help prove I'm telling the truth." She held up a small round crystal etched with glowing runes. "A list of all Orla's allies."

Ed tightened his grip on her hand. *You're right we should go. I don't like this.*

I'm glad you finally agree with me. Ann traced runes in the air, muttering words of power to transport them out of the building. Light flashed around them, enveloping their bodies.

As it did, Ceara threw the crystal toward them. Thunder roared as an explosion ripped through the air.

Ann screamed as the transference spell wrenched her body away and she felt Ed's hand let go of hers.

She landed hard outside the bunker, the air leaving her lungs in a *whoosh.*

Ann scrambled up, ignoring the wave of dizziness as she ran back inside. But when she reached the meeting room, Ed and Ceara were gone.

CHAPTER 1

Three months later

"Are you sure this is the right place?" Ann asked her brother as they walked into a deserted alley situated between two tall steel buildings. "I want to know more about this person." She guessed the buildings must have been warehouses, but it was hard to tell. Not many people knew much about the ruins left over from ancient times. Back then, Erthea had had technology, but she had heard things in tales. The warehouses had broken glass windows, and their steel had long since rusted with age.

"This is where she said we'd find the person we're supposed to help," Xander replied. "Sage wants us to find them and get them to safety." He pulled his cloak tighter as the cool night breeze ruffled his short dark hair. With grey eyes and black hair, he reminded her so much of their mother.

"Did she say who they were? Or why we're helping them?" It wasn't unusual for Sage to help people who were being hunted, especially suspected magic users in Caselhelm. "We need to be extra careful." After losing Edward, she didn't want to risk anything happening to Xander.

Being so close to the border between Caselhelm and Asral made Ann uneasy. Although she and Xander were protected and had new identities, she knew the people who murdered their parents were still looking for them. Just because five years had passed didn't mean they were any safer.

Ann tapped her foot against the wall they sat on. She hadn't been able to find any trace of Edward since the night she'd last seen him. Xander seemed to have given up hope, but Ann knew deep down he was still alive. He had to be, and she wouldn't give up until she found him. She'd know if he were dead. Somehow, she'd feel it.

"She said they were being hunted by Gliss but didn't give any further details."

Ann glanced over at him and frowned. "What happens after we save them and fend off the Gliss?" she asked. "Do we help them get to Trin?" She didn't much like the idea of returning to the druids' isle. It always felt bittersweet going back there. "And how do we know this isn't another trap like the last time Sage set up a meeting?"

Sage hadn't been any help with finding Ed either.

Xander shrugged. "Don't know. I'm surprised she asked us, given Edward..." his voice trailed off.

"Given Ed isn't around anymore. You can say it." She looked away, the familiar ache heavy in her chest at the thought of him.

Xander shivered. "Remind me why I had to come along? You know I'm not much help when it comes to fighting Gliss."

"Because you need to get out of that library for a while. It's not good for you being cooped up in there all the time."

"Hey, I leave every day, and—"

"And go to the tavern every night to hook up with different women." Ann rolled her eyes. "Living in hiding means we're not supposed to reveal ourselves, brother."

"Says the woman who goes out helping persecuted magic users every chance she gets," Xander said. "That's hardly keeping a low profile either, *sister.*"

"When Orla proclaimed all magic users not in her select circle should be put to death, I had to do something! I can't work in a library all the time. I need action."

"Now you sound like Papa. He lived for action."

"He didn't have much choice, did he?" Ann winced at the mention of their father, forcing down the grief that threatened to overtake her. "There's no sign of anyone. Are you sure the message came from Sage?" It wouldn't be the first time the Gliss tried to trick them. Ann cast her senses out, scanning the surrounding area for any signs of life. If Ceara thought she could lead them into another trap, she'd be damn wrong. Still, Ann wanted to get her hands on that bloody Gliss again and force her to tell them what she'd done with Ed.

"Maybe they're not coming. It's too bloody cold." Xander fidgeted.

Ann's cool blue eyes narrowed as she pulled up her hood. She wouldn't let him know that the cold bothered her too. "You are such a baby at times. Sometimes I wonder how you ever passed basic druid training."

Above them, stars glittered like tiny diamonds in the darkness. Ann hoped they wouldn't have to stick around here for much longer. She hated being out in the open like this. It made her feel vulnerable and exposed. A chill ran down her spine that had nothing to do with the icy air. Ann leapt down from the wall she'd been sitting on, landing several feet below in the alley and pulling out her short sword. "Company."

A man came running down the alleyway. She caught a flash of his glowing emerald eyes as he ran past her. Okay, she hadn't been expecting that. What was that creature? Another monster sent by Orla to attack them?

Behind him came three women dressed in dark brown leathers—Gliss. The Gliss were empaths who had been trained to use their gifts to harm others. Instead of healing emotional pain like most empaths, they used their powers to project emotions and memories onto their victims. Ann knew first-hand how painful it could be having your emotions and powers reflected back at you. But she'd learned to use her mental shield to block it out to an extent.

Perfect. Oh well, time to party.

The strange beast-man vanished in the opposite direction. Surely, this couldn't be the person they were meant to help? If so, Sage had gone batty.

Xander jumped down beside her, pulling out his staff. "That must be the person we're supposed to save. Why—?"

"Guess we'd better help him." Ann gripped her sword. "Hey!" She raised her hand and threw a fireball at one of the Gliss.

The Gliss stumbled forward then spun around, pulling out one of her throwing knives.

Ann dodged it, responding with another fireball. The Gliss raised a gloved hand to deflect back at her.

Ducking out of its path, Ann grabbed the knife now embedded in the wall behind her and hurled it at the Gliss. It struck the woman's head, knocking her to the ground, dead.

Xander fired his staff, sending out a bolt of blue lightning as the second Gliss came at him. She slumped to the floor, unconscious.

Ann could never understand why Xander preferred to use makeshift weapons instead of magic. He wasn't as powerless as he believed himself to be. She knelt to slit the woman's throat. She didn't like to kill but couldn't leave a Gliss alive. As Ann drew closer, the woman's eyes flew open, and she grabbed Ann by the throat. Ann gasped as the woman started strangling her with her own magic. A Gliss' touch was much harder to fight against at close range than if they used their power from a distance.

Something blurred as the man with emerald eyes reappeared, yanking the Gliss away from Ann and snapping her neck in one swift move.

The third Gliss, who had taken over fighting Xander, flew at the man, thrusting a blade through his back.

Running over to Ann, Xander helped her up. "You alright?"

"Fine." She grabbed the knife from the head of the first fallen Gliss, preparing to kill the third.

But before Ann could reach her, the beast-man, grunting from the pain, spun and ripped the woman's head off her shoulders. He then sank to his knees.

Ann hurried over to him, pulling the knife out of his back and turning him over to examine the wound. To her surprise, it didn't look as bad as she'd expected. It had turned pink around the edges, as though it had already begun to heal.

She turned him back over, to her amazement, his fangs and claws had retracted. Now they'd vanished, it revealed a man with long brown hair, a muscular body, and rough stubble. "Ed," she gasped. "How is this possible?" She couldn't believe it. He was alive. He'd finally come back. Part of her wanted to wrap her arms around him and ask him where he'd been, but that'd have to wait until later.

Xander came over. "Is it really him? How could he have survived the explosion?"

Ann clutched Ed's arm and scanned his body with her mind. She couldn't make out any of his thoughts; they were a jumbled mess of confusion. Strange, she'd been able to read his thoughts more easily than anyone else—sometimes without even meaning to. Ann would scan his mind deeper later, even his immediate injuries would have to wait until they were safe.

"It's him. We need to get him back to the warehouse. His wounds need tending." She rose and pulled out a vial, tipping some of its contents over each of the Gliss' bodies. "Let's get out of here. More could show up, and we don't want to be here when they do."

"Bain amach agus scrios iad." She recited words of power, and the whole alley flashed with white light as it removed any lingering traces of their magic and the bodies evaporated.

"Let's go." She slipped one arm under Ed's shoulder while Xander took the other.

Xander grunted. "Maybe we shouldn't go back to the warehouse, they might be able to track us there. We should just—"

"Are you suggesting we leave him here to die?" Ann stared at her brother in disbelief.

"He's not Edward anymore, I don't know who he is now. He might be even more of a threat to us than the—" He sighed. "Think about it, Ann. Ed wouldn't want to put us in danger by bringing Gliss our way. Orla could be using him to get to us. You have no idea what she might have done to him."

She glared at Xander, raising her chin. "He's our friend. I'm not leaving him again."

Together they dragged Ed all the way back to the warehouse

they'd been staying in for the last month. Being on the run rarely gave them a chance to live in real houses anymore and living in abandoned buildings was easier. That way, they drew little attention to themselves and didn't get asked unwanted questions. They never stayed in one place for long, either.

They pulled Ed onto Xander's makeshift bed, which sat in the far corner away from the dripping pipes and piles of rubbish they had accumulated during their time there.

Ann cut off Ed's shredded shirt, gasping when she saw the scars covering his body. "What did they do you?" she whispered.

When she examined the stab wound on his back, she realised it had started to close over. "He's healing faster than even a druid could."

"Guess that's something else unusual about him," Xander remarked. "Ann, I don't think we should have brought him back here."

"Sage sent us to help him." Ann didn't want to believe Ed could be used against them. "I'll tend to his wounds."

"The Gliss were chasing him. If they track him—"

"Then we'll be ready for them," she said. "Now go outside and start setting the wards."

CHAPTER 2

Ann cleaned the wound, applied some healing ointment, then bandaged it. Ed remained unconscious throughout. Her mind raced with questions she desperately wanted to ask him.

What had happened to him? What had he turned into? And why?

She knew from the scars covering his body he'd been tortured. It could only have been at Orla's hands. Despite all the different forces fighting over Caselhelm, the northernmost realm out of the five lands, only Orla would be so interested in getting her claws into one of Darius' elite warriors.

Back during her father's rule, the Black Guard had been the best warriors in the five lands. Trained in both weapons and different forms of magic.

Light flashed through the plate-glass windows as Xander placed protective wards outside. The wards cast eerie pools of green light around the warehouse. They would at least slow down any potential attackers and warn them of danger.

Xander came back in, frowning. "Has he woken up?" He glanced over to where Ed lay on a pile of blankets.

She shook her head. "No, but he's healing. I think he'll be okay."

"Have you tried calling Sage?" Xander slumped down onto a small wooden chair they had salvaged from the warehouse's debris.

Ann scoffed. She'd rather not talk to Sage, even at the best of times. "No, have you?" She slipped a blanket over Edward. She didn't want to talk to Sage, in thought or in person.

"I tried, but she isn't answering."

Typical Sage. Send orders first, answer questions never.

"We need to move. It's not safe for us here now," Xander said.

"Agreed, but I think we should wait until first light. Let Ed rest for a few hours."

"I meant without him."

"We can't leave him; he's our friend." She crossed her arms. She wouldn't leave Ed behind, no matter what Xander said. Ann couldn't believe he would even suggest such a thing. Ed had been their friend for most of their lives. He had stuck by them through everything.

"We haven't seen him in months. How do you know Orla didn't send him to find us?" Xander retorted. "I expected you of all people to be more suspicious. Have you even checked him over to see if he has any traces on him?"

Ann hesitated. She'd been too concerned with his injuries and wondering what might have happened to him. *Stupid,* she told herself. *I'm getting sloppy.* They couldn't afford to be sloppy.

She placed her hand on Ed's forehead, scanning his body for any traces of magic. "I don't sense anything."

Ann closed her eyes, willing her mind to probe deeper into his body as she scanned him for injuries and threats. Aside from the wound to his back, she could find no other physical damage. Even the scars felt like they were healing.

Ed, can you hear me? She waited, expecting to feel him stir. She sensed it then, another presence at the edge of his mind. It felt raw, powerful, and unlike anything she'd sensed before. *What is that?*

Before she had a chance to probe further, the presence disappeared.

Xander finished checking Ed's body for any physical traces of magic and gathered up some of his books. "We should still leave now." They only had a few meagre possessions. His included books, a few instruments and devices. Life on the run gave them little time to pack up when they needed to make a quick exit.

"I'm not leaving him. Sage wanted us to help him, and we will." Ann decided against telling Xander about the strange presence she'd felt in Ed's mind. *It's too soon to tell what it is or if it's a threat.* Plus, she didn't want to give Xander any more reason to distrust Ed.

"Since when do you defend Sage?" Xander raised an eyebrow.

"I may not like the old bat, but she's right about some things. Don't you want to know what happened to him?" she demanded. "He's our oldest friend. We can't abandon him." She couldn't bear the thought of leaving Ed behind again.

"Aren't you afraid of what he is now?" Xander shoved the books into his pack.

Ann glanced down at Ed's unconscious form. She knew she should be afraid, but all she felt was relief. "We'll take him to Trin. That's the safest place for us. Maybe Sage or Aunt Flo can help him."

"Maybe you should stop letting your feelings for him cloud your better judgement."

Her mouth fell open. "My what? I don't—"

"Come on, Annie. You've got to—"

"Enough," Ann snapped, stalking over to the other side of the room and grabbing her pillow. "I'm getting some sleep. I suggest you do the same."

Xander only shook his head and stormed outside, muttering something about checking the perimeter.

Ann settled down next to Ed, pulling her cloak over her like a blanket. "You have a lot of explaining to do," she murmured to him before sinking into an uneasy sleep.

The next thing she knew, someone shook her awake.

"Wake up, it's past dawn," Xander said. "We need to get moving."

Ann rubbed the sleep from her eyes as she sat up. Pale shafts of sunlight crept in through the warehouse's windows, casting faint pools of green light over the stone floor. The air smelt damp and stale. She'd be glad to get out of this place and find somewhere new to live for a while. Where didn't matter. As long she had her brother and Ed, she'd be happy to sleep in a pigsty.

Ed still lay at her side, unmoving. She checked his back, saw the stab wound had faded to a jagged pink scar. His older scars had faded, too.

Incredible. She'd never seen any Magickind heal so fast before; most healing magic took days to fix serious injuries. It only made her more curious to find out what Orla had done to him. Most Magickind didn't have glowing emerald eyes, either.

Xander stood in the corner, shaking a vial from the potion kit that he used to test different types of spells and magic.

"What are you doing?" Ann scrambled out of bed and stood, running a hand through her hair.

"Testing his blood. It doesn't look natural," he remarked. "Hurry up and pack your things. We need to get moving."

She glanced over at Ed. "We'll wake him up when we're ready—"

"I still think it's a bad idea to take him with us," Xander remarked. "No one heals that fast, not even one of the Black. I don't know what does. It'd be safer if we just left without him."

Ann's eyes flashed, and she put her hands on her hips. "We've already had this conversation. We'll ask him about it when he wakes up."

Ann washed, bathing in the icy water coming through a rusty pipe that brought rainwater down from the roof. She changed into her usual black leather trousers and black tunic. She put her weapons, sleeping mat, pillow and few meagre possessions into a large pack.

When she had finished, Ed still hadn't woken. It looked like he hadn't moved all night.

Ann shook his shoulder. "Ed? Time to wake up."

Ed's hand shot up, grasping Ann by the throat as he jolted awake.

"Ed…it's me, Ann." She raised her hand, ready to use her magic if she had to. *Please don't make me hurt you.*

Xander grabbed hold of her short sword and raised it. "Edward, let go of my sister, or I will kill you."

Ed let go of her, making Ann cough from where he'd gripped her so hard. Instead, he flew at Xander, knocking the sword from his

31

grasp. He pinned Xander against the wall, squeezing his throat so hard Xander's eyes bulged.

"Ed, no, stop!" Ann rushed over to grab his arm. "Don't hurt him. Listen to me, you can't hurt him."

Ed's blazing emerald eyes turned toward her, and he pulled back, letting Xander fall to the ground. Xander coughed, clutching his throat.

Ed's dark gaze narrowed, but there was a flash of recognition in them. "Ann?" he rasped, drawing his hand away. "What…? I'm so sorry. Did I hurt you?" He looked down at Xander. "Are you both alright?"

"I'm fine." Her throat ached from where he'd gripped her so hard, but she forced a smile. "Welcome back, we've missed you. How do you feel?"

He rubbed the back of his head, then shook it, dazed. "I-I don't know. Where are we?"

"We are close to Caselhelm, in a place called Noridge," Xander replied and scrambled up "What in the name of the spirits happened to you? What *are* you?" He glared at Ed. "I can't believe you'd attack us." He swung around to face his sister. "I told you he's a danger to

32

us now. We should—"

We're not going to hurt him, Ann snapped. *We don't know what Orla turned him into. But there's no way we're turning our back on him. Not now. We finally have him back.*

Ed shook his head. "I don't know."

"Xander, why don't you go get us some breakfast from town? We could use some extra supplies."

Xander stared at her in disbelief. "He just attacked us, and you want me to get breakfast? What is wrong with you?"

Ann silenced him in thought. *Go. We'll leave when you get back. He's been through a lot, let me talk to him.*

He tried to kill you! Xander kept a tight grip on her sword, eying Ed as if expecting him to attack again.

He didn't mean to. Plus, he won't hurt me, I know it. It's not as if he can kill me, even if he did try. Ann crossed her arms.

We don't have time to waste, Annie.

Go. She glared at him. *I'll talk to him and find out what happened. If he does prove to be a threat, we will deal with it.*

"If you hurt her, I will kill you," he growled at Ed. "I'm not blinded by emotion like she is," Xander muttered a curse and stalked

33

off.

"Ed, you need to tell me what happened to you," she said. "How did they–?"

Ed covered his ears and doubled over. "Argh, why is everything is so loud? Make it stop."

Ann frowned. All she heard was the drip of the pipes and the faint groan of metal from the ancient building. Ed acted like thunder boomed around them. What had those wretched Gliss done to him? Maybe it had something to do with the wolf-like beast they had transformed him into.

"It's okay." She touched his arm.

He flinched as if her touch pained him. "Don't touch me," he growled.

Ann tried to think of a way to help him, her mind racing with spells. She chanted one, feeling her power carry on the air as she tried to soothe him. "*A bheith socair.*"

Ed frowned and scrambled up. "What did you do?"

"Something to calm you. Feel better?"

He nodded and wrapped his arms around her, burying his head against her shoulder. "Ann, what's happening to me? Everything is blurry, but I feel like I haven't seen you in months."

Her eyes widened. Ann couldn't remember him holding her like this—not for a long time, at least. She returned the embrace, enjoying the feel of his warm skin. "It's okay, you're safe." She knew they had to get moving, but part of her didn't want to let him go. "We have to get to Trin. There will be Gliss looking for you."

"Gliss?" His frown deepened, almost as if he didn't know what they were. "Ann, what's happening to me?" he said again.

"I don't know, but we'll figure it out," she admitted. "I'll find you some clothes, then we must get moving."

CHAPTER 3

Edward blinked, his mind racing with unanswered questions as he tried to make sense of his jumbled mess of thoughts. He had no idea how he had ended up here. Every time he tried to focus on what happened to him, the hazier it became.

"What's the last thing you remember?" Ann asked as she handed him a pair of black trousers and a rough grey linen shirt.

"We were talking to Ceara," he said, smiling as the picture formed in his mind. "She said she wanted to talk to the council of elders to help prove your innocence." Relief washed over him. Maybe his memories were coming back.

"What about after that?"

He rubbed his chin. "I don't know. You started to transport us out of there. I remember being blinded by light…running through the darkness. Then I saw you in the alleyway."

"We met with Ceara three months ago," Ann told him. "After I started to transport us, Ceara threw a crystal. There was an explosion, and we got separated. I searched everywhere for you but couldn't find you. We thought you were dead."

"Three months…" Ed murmured. That seemed impossible. Where had he been for three months? What had he done? He shook his head. "How can that be?"

"It's probably just trauma making you forget. The Gliss do terrible things to prisoners." She hesitated. "Ed, they—"

As the door creaked open, the screech made him wince, but things weren't as loud as when he'd first woken up. Xander walked in, carrying a small sack. The smell of pastries and fresh bread emanating from inside it made Ed's mouth water. Hunger gnawed at his stomach. Spirits only knew how long it had been since he'd eaten.

"I've got supplies," Xander said. "Let's get moving."

"I'm relieved you stayed safe while I was gone," Ed remarked.

Xander glanced over at Ed. "We'll get you to Trin, but then you're on your own."

Ed frowned, surprised by his hostility. Was Xander angry at him for being gone so long? Ann hadn't reacted that way. He somehow missed the feel of their closeness and wanted to pull her back into his arms. He wondered where the feeling had come from.

"Get dressed. We need to get moving," Xander ordered. "Ann, come help me perform a cleansing and make sure we don't leave anything behind."

Ed showered, wincing at the icy water on his skin, then changed into fresh clothes. It made him feel a little better. But he still felt strange, different. Everything seemed brighter and louder somehow, and he couldn't understand why.

Xander scoured the warehouse, checking for anything the Gliss could use to track them with. He used cleansing spells to remove any traces of their magic.

Maybe going to Trin and seeing Sage–one of the few members of the druid order–would shed some light on what had happened to him. She might not be powerful like Ann, but she had decades of knowledge and experience.

"Are you sure you're alright to travel?" Ann asked Ed. "A Gliss stabbed you last night."

"Stabbed? Where?" He ran his hands under his shirt, checking for any signs of injury. But found nothing except a tender spot on his back. He glanced at Ann. "Did you heal me?"

"No, you did that yourself. Your body is healing at an abnormal rate."

"Can we please get moving?" Xander demanded, leaning against the wall. "There are probably Gliss nearby, and—"

Silver flashed as a knife came whirling through the air, hitting Xander in the shoulder.

A Gliss appeared, flanked by two others. All were dressed in brown leather.

Ed ducked and pulled Ann down with him as several knives flew at them. He shot to his feet, lunging at the first Gliss. She came at him with a knife that curved into three different blades. He blocked the blow, knocking the blade away as he caught hold of her wrist, twisting it and feeling the snap of bone. While the pain incapacitated her, he snapped her neck in one swift move.

Ann grabbed one of the fallen knives, flinging it at the second Gliss.

The woman dodged it, and Ed grabbed her. The Gliss jabbed a knife at him, grazing his face. He looked down, surprised to see his fingers replaced by claws as he moved to disarm her. Staring her straight in the eye, he saw his own reflection shining back, and realised his eyes were glowing a deep shade of emerald. What did it mean?

Catching hold of her hair, he wrenched her head off her shoulders in one swift move.

The only remaining Gliss snarled and lunged at him.

He blocked her blow, spun, and snapped her neck. She slumped to the ground, dead.

Blood now covered his hands and the claws that stuck out from them. He stared around at the carnage he'd caused. He couldn't believe what he'd just done. As one of the Black, killing people to protect others wasn't new to him. Still, he'd never brutally slaughtered anyone like this before. When he had to kill, it was usually by a sword, not with his bare hands in such a savage manner.

Blood pounded in his ears. What had he done? What was he? He turned and caught his reflection again. This time in a small puddle of water. His eyes still glowed deep emerald and fangs now protruded from his mouth. He looked like a beast.

"Ed, where's Xander?" Ann moved past him.

Ed blinked, still feeling dazed. He stared down at the broken and bloodied bodies of the Gliss. *What have I done? What have I become?*

"He's not here. Xander? Xander!" Ann hurried outside. "Ed, help me."

Ed shook his head, stunned by what he'd done.

"Edward!"

He walked outside, the sun's rays stinging his eyes as the glare from the light blinded him. Looking up, the sun appeared to be hidden behind heavy clouds. Why did it seem so bright?

"Xander's gone. I thought I saw someone outside before they knocked me out," she said. "Damn it, they must have taken him. How could they have known we were here?"

"You didn't seem shocked by what I just did," he remarked,

searching her face for a reaction. He looked at his claws again. They were long, black, and sharp.

Damn, how do I get rid of these things?

"You did the same last night. You moved and fought in a way I've never seen before."

"What did they do to me?"

"It doesn't matter. We have to find Xander. If Orla has him—"

Ed took a deep breath, forcing himself to become calm. His claws retracted. "We have to get to Trin." His panic and horror at what he'd done faded as instinct took over. He still had a duty to keep Ann safe, and he wouldn't let anything get in the way of that.

"No, we have to search was Xander. He might—"

"We both know he's long gone. They would have whisked him to another location. We can't go after them. They could be miles from here by now." Ed grabbed a piece of discarded cloth and wiped some of the blood off his hands. He noticed it splattered over his shirt and gritted his teeth. "*Glan,*" he muttered, waiting. After a few moments, the specks of blood disappeared. Ed breathed a sigh of relief. Perhaps his magic wasn't gone as he'd feared.

"Why did you have to come back?" Ann cried. "We were safe. We were—"

"Ann." He gripped her shoulders. "I swear I'll do everything I can help you find him. Right now, my first priority is keeping you safe. More Gliss will be coming. We need to move." He grabbed Xander's pack and handed Ann hers.

Her eyes narrowed. "How do I know you're not a danger to me now?" she hissed. "You're not a druid anymore, you're different. You killed those Gliss without blinking."

"It doesn't matter what I am now, I know I would never hurt you. You have to trust me on that." In truth, he had never considered himself a druid. Although they had raised him, he knew his own powers and abilities were different. "Besides, I've never been a real druid."

"No, I'm not leaving without searching for my brother first. He's the only close family I have left," Ann said, raising her hands. "*Rhombus.*"

A glowing field of energy flared around Ed, repelling him when he made a move toward her. He muttered a curse as Ann took off in the opposite direction.

Bugger. He raised his hands, calling on the elements around him.

For several moments, nothing happened. Had he lost his magic along with his memories?

Ed spotted the black silhouette of Ann's disappearing form and felt a rush of anger. She'd get herself killed, and he wouldn't be there to stop it. Although he couldn't blame her for being angry—he'd led the Gliss straight to them just by being here.

His body blurred as he shot through the circle, its energy prickling his skin. Colour whirled past him as he moved, and he felt a dizzying rush of energy.

He reappeared standing in front of her. "Ann, stop," he said, breathing hard. "I don't know what happened to me, but you know I'm your friend. My orders are to keep you safe from the Gliss. I can't do that if you run from me."

"You didn't do a very good job, did you? Xander is gone." Her eyes flashed with anger.

"We'll get him back," he said. "But first we need Sage. She'll know how to proceed." Despite everything that happened to him, he couldn't stand the thought of losing Ann as well. He knew what Xander being gone would do to her. He had to keep the promise he had made to her father.

Even if it cost him his life.

CHAPTER 4

Xander opened his eyes and blinked a few times. The back of his neck stung from where something had struck him. His head throbbed; bile rose in his throat. What happened? He remembered being in the warehouse with Ann and Ed. They'd been talking, arguing over their next move, when the Gliss had burst in.

The darkness was pierced by bright orange light. It burnt his eyes, making him look aware as his vision adjusted to the glare.

"Hello, Xander," said a female voice that sounded familiar.

A woman with long black hair, pale skin and dark eyes stared down at him.

No, it can't be her...

Xander blinked again. "Ceara…" Her form wavered. He made a move to reach up and grasp his aching head but couldn't. His arms were shackled behind the wooden chair he sat on.

As his eyes adjusted to the low light, the room came into view. There was a stone floor covered in dirt, littered with dark stains— blood?— as well as flickering torches on the wall. Devices hung from the walls and ceiling. A slab of stone covered a large hole in the floor. Xander had seen such things in other temples and knew they were used in torture.

"It's been a long time," Ceara said. "Have you missed me?"

He glared at her. "No, you betrayed me by having an affair with my brother, remember?" he spat. "Where am I? Where are Edward and Ann?"

"That's none of your concern." Ceara waved a dismissive hand. "You—"

A wave of dizziness rolled over him, and bile rose in his throat once again. He shut his mouth and closed his eyes, blocking out her words.

When he reached for his magic, nothing happened. No doubt the shackles bound it. That meant he wouldn't be able to contact Ann to find out if she and Ed were okay. He prayed to the spirits they'd escaped.

Xander couldn't believe he'd been captured when the Gliss had come into the warehouse. After years of looking over his shoulder and being careful, he'd fallen right into Orla's hands.

Worse still, here was Ceara. The woman he once loved who'd betrayed him. She'd helped Orla murder his parents and destroy Caselhelm.

He remembered seeing Ed change, ripping a Gliss apart. He had no idea what Ed was now, but he would keep Ann safe. That thought gave him some comfort. Ann would look for him, he knew her, but she had to stay away.

It's too dangerous for her to come for me.

A hard slap brought him out of his thoughts. Xander winced and opened his eyes again, forcing himself to look at Ceara. She looked just as he remembered. Same dark eyes, same cold beauty. How he loved her once. He would have done anything for her.

"Are you even listening to me?" she demanded.

Xander shook his head. "Sorry if I'm suffering from where you struck me."

Ceara snorted. "You're the son of the archdruid—*former* archdruid. I doubt a blow to the head would do you much damage."

"What do you want, Ceara?" Xander demanded. "I doubt you changed your mind and realised you picked the wrong brother. So out with it."

"Orla will be here soon, and you won't like what she has in mind for you," Ceara said, touching his forehead. Her hand flared with light, white light radiating from her own forehead as her magic pulsed through him.

Xander braced himself for the inevitable pain. He wasn't like Ann. He didn't have her strength, training or power, and his own earth affinity had always been weak.

"Tell me what happened to Urien."

That's it? He should have known she'd captured him to find his elder half-brother. After all, she had chosen Urien over him.

"He's dead. Ann killed him after he murdered our father."

"Lies. I know he's still alive, probably trapped somewhere in spirit form," she snapped.

"You're wasting your time. How would I know what happened? I was already dead, remember?" Xander snapped back. "You stabbed me, *killed* me." He glared at her. For years after his 'death', he had thought about her. He'd wondered how different life would have been if she had chosen him instead of Urien. Now he felt no love for her. "Even if I knew what happened to Urien, I wouldn't tell you. The last thing the five lands need is for my bastard brother to reunite with his demon mother."

The sound of heavy footsteps echoed down the hall, and power crackled in the air.

"Xander, believe it or not, I'm trying to help you," Ceara told him.

"Just like you helped by turning Edward into a beast?" he said. "Go away, we have nothing to say to each other."

"Orla will torture you. You know that."

Voices echoed from outside the chamber. Ceara leaned down and hissed in his ear, "Please tell me where Urien is. Then I won't have to hurt you. Please, Xander."

Strange. She almost sounded sincere.

Xander wouldn't believe a word that came out of her mouth. *It's a trick,* he told himself. *She played with your emotions before, she'll do it again.*

The door creaked open and in walked a tall, lithe woman with black and cobalt blue hair. Piercing blue eyes flecked with gold told him she was a Fomorian demon. The druids had defeated the Fomorians during one of the many realm wars. But now Orla had control of druid lands.

Xander's stomach twisted as he stared at his father's former mistress—the woman who'd killed his sweet, gentle mother.

"Alexander, you're not the one I expected." Orla gave Ceara a hard look. "You were supposed to bring Rhiannon, not him."

"We tried to grab her, but—" Ceara shook her head.

Hearing Ann had escaped, Xander felt a rush of hope.

Ceara and Orla fell silent, no doubt arguing mentally as they glared at each other.

Xander tugged at his restraints, but they held firm. He had to find a way out of here, to get a message to his sister.

Orla turned her steely gaze back to him. "Maybe you can prove useful after all." She moved closer. "You and Rhiannon are close. She would have told you what she did to Urien."

"What makes you think she's still alive?" Xander demanded. "It's been five years. We've been hunted by more than you. Or do you forget the enormous price we have on our heads?"

Orla laughed. "Your glamour is good. I know she's still alive," she said. "Tell me what happened to my son."

"Urien is dead. You and Ceara need to accept that." Xander raised his chin in a show of courage he didn't have. He knew they'd torture him, but he'd get through it, somehow. He tried to fight the cold sliver of fear that went down his spine.

It will be alright. You can't tell them what you don't know.

Orla hit him so hard his head reeled back, making him see stars. "My Gliss can give you pain beyond imagining. I know you, Xander, I know you're the weak one of Darius' children." She leaned closer. "Tell me where Urien is."

Xander shook his head. "I don't know."

Orla produced a small metal rod and pressed it against his neck. Heat seared his skin, sending shockwaves through his body. He closed his eyes and clamped his mouth shut to keep from crying out. When it wasn't producing lightning, the magic in the rod magnified pain. Orla pressed it harder into his skin, sending pain shooting through every nerve ending.

Xander's eyes watered as tears flowed down his cheeks. *Ann. Think of getting back to her.*

His ears rang as Orla pulled back. "You'll only cause yourself more pain."

Xander looked up. "You'll never find Urien. He's dead, and he will stay that way."

"Ceara, go into his mind," Orla ordered.

Ceara's eyes widened. "What? He's not been broken yet. My magic won't be able to—"

"I don't have time for the usual methods. Use your power to break him."

Xander looked up. Weren't they supposed to weaken his body to make his mind more pliable?

"He's a Valeran. What if I can't read him?" she asked.

Xander stared at her, wondering why she stalled for time. They both knew her powers worked on him. She'd used them for pleasure when they were together.

"Do it," Orla snapped, slapping Ceara so hard her hand came

away bloody.

He met her gaze, thinking he saw a hint of something there. Sadness? No, she didn't care for him and never had.

Ceara wiped her lip with the back of her gloved hand and moved to his side as Orla stepped back. Ceara hesitated as she pulled off her leather gloves. Direct contact made it easier for Gliss to unleash their power.

"Ceara," Orla snapped. "We don't have…" She quieted as Ceara caressed the side of Xander's face.

He flinched, surprised when her power didn't hit against him.

Light flared on Ceara's forehead, extending out as she placed a hand on either side of his head. Her magic pulsed through him, burning like white-hot fire.

This time, he screamed.

CHAPTER 5

Ann ran a hand through her hair as she and Ed moved up a steep embankment. They'd covered a good five miles in the past few hours, thanks to transference. Ed hadn't said much during that time, and she didn't say anything either. The fear she'd fought to keep locked away for years had started to unravel. They were close to the south-eastern edge of Caselhelm, near The Whispering Tops, mountains that bordered Asral and Lulrien. Their magnificent high peaks looked like grey giants whose eyes were forever watching. Ann had never liked those mountains. A lot of people went missing up there, but luckily the road to Trin didn't require going over them.

Keep it together, she told herself. But all thoughts of Orla made her think of her parents. She pushed all memories of her dead parents away. The last thing she needed to remember was their murder, or to wonder what Orla might be doing to her brother.

"Orla won't kill him," Ed broke the silence to voice her thoughts. "She needs him to get what she wants."

Xander can't die, she reminded herself.

Their father had seen to that by casting a spell that bound his children together. Now, neither she nor Xander could die, no matter how badly they were injured. Ann suspected he'd done it to stop Urien from killing her. She still wished her father would've told her about the spell, about so many things that he'd never had the chance to tell her.

But she didn't worry for her brother's life, she worried about what Orla might learn from him. If Orla found what she wanted, the five lands would be doomed.

"He can't die," Ann remarked. "When she figures that out, she'll keep killing him to get what she wants." She shuddered at the thought. *It doesn't matter what the Gliss do to him. He doesn't know anything.*

Orla and Urien had created the Gliss to be Orla's own version of the Black Guard.

"She won't find the key again. We made sure of that," Ed said.

"She can try. Orla has spent years trying to find Urien's power. Xander and I having new identities won't stop that," she said, giving him a hard look. "Do you really not remember how you were turned into a beast?"

Ed shook his head. "I don't remember any of it. I'm just as shocked as you are." He paused. "I can't use all of my magic anymore. I feel like my soul has been put into a different body—one I don't recognise."

Ann glanced off into the distance as mist rolled over the ancient mountains. "No one's followed us. I'd say we're safe to perform another transference now." She knelt, drawing runes on the ground, then a circle. She stepped inside but hesitated.

The man she'd known for most of her life felt like a stranger to her. Could she trust him? She'd been so happy to have him back she'd ignored Xander's suspicions. If he did prove to be a threat, what would she do then? Those closest to her had betrayed her once before. She didn't think she'd survive if Edward turned against her, too. He'd been by her side even through the plot for power that cost her both her home and her family.

Now she didn't know what to think. What if she was taking an enemy into one of the few safe havens left? Trin was a sacred island to the druids, one of the few places in Almara that Orla and the other rulers hadn't managed to conquer.

"Ann, you and I have known each other for a long time. You know I'd never do anything to hurt you," Ed said, reading her mind again. She hated when he did that and raised her mental shield to block him out. The connection that had once been so natural between them now felt like a violation.

"I did once, but now I can't be sure." She wanted to trust him, but he'd changed—everything had—and saving him had cost her Xander. "You don't even know what you are. We have no idea what the Gliss might have done to you. Orla will stop at nothing to get what she wants; she'd even use you against me."

"I didn't attack you, did I?" Ed said. "If I prove to be any kind of danger, I'll leave. I still have a duty to you." He caressed her cheek. "More than that, I don't want to leave you."

Ann's heart twisted at the mention of him leaving. Before the last three months, they'd rarely been apart during the fifteen years they'd known each other. Losing him would be like losing another member of what little family she'd left.

Reluctantly, she held out her hand. He took it and stepped inside the circle. She chanted words of power, and the runes around them flashed bright amber. Flames rose from within the circle, enveloping them both. Ann felt the familiar dizzying whoosh of the transference taking her and Ed to another place. Light danced around her in a rush of stars and colours as they moved.

Ann and Ed reappeared a few seconds later on the edge of a river. The river looked like a pale blue mirror, its water so calm there was no movement. The air smelt rich with the scent of salt and the sharp sea lilies that grew along the bank, their pale petals arching in a cylindrical shape. Ann looked along the edge of the shore, sending her mind along the river that gave way to the Eastern Sea. She felt no other presences nearby except for Edward, who stood beside her.

This entire area had once been part of the mainland. It had been swallowed up by magical mist, creating a veil that kept Trin hidden from prying eyes.

Ed still seemed on edge, she noticed. He kept glancing in every direction and rubbed his ears and eyes a couple of times. She couldn't imagine what his newly heightened senses must be doing to him. Ann considered trying to use a spell to help him keep it under control, but it would have to wait until they reached the island. She didn't have time to cast a spell out in the open like this. Ann would try to help him if she could, but in truth, she had no idea if her magic would even work.

Without thinking, Ann touched his shoulder. He flinched, surprised by the action. "It will be alright. We'll figure out what this beast is."

Ed shook his head. Saying nothing, he walked to the edge of the bank and started pulling back the heavy reeds, muttering words of power. Ann sensed it in the air as the dark reeds twisted and bent.

"Maybe I should…" Ann said. The reeds rose, twisting together until they formed a small boat, large enough to carry two people. Two seats formed across the centre of the boat, giving them places to sit down.

"See? Your magic isn't gone." That relieved her. Maybe the beast hadn't managed to take full control yet, and she could still coax it out of him when they reached the island.

"That's easy magic. A child could do it." Ed shook his head. "No, my power is different now." He picked up a small log, which split in half as he flexed it between his fingers. It splintered away like dust. He muttered more words of power, and an oar made of woven reeds formed inside the boat.

The island's magic still amazed Ann. She'd been fascinated by it since the first time her father, Darius, had brought her to the here as a child. That memory was one of the reasons why she hated going back. The island reminded her so much of him, of the people and the life she'd lost.

Ann climbed into the boat and sat. She half expected the reeds to fall away and go crashing into the water. The boat held firm and watertight, rocking back and forth against the gentle waves.

Ed climbed in the other end, and they paddled away from shore. The mist around them grew heavier, surrounding them like a thick blanket as they moved further out into the water. It had been created centuries ago to keep one of the druids' last places of refuge safe. The mist hummed against her skin, heavy with ancient magic that called to her own powers. All druids had an affinity for different elements. Anyone who tried sailing through the mist would be diverted unless they knew where to go. The mist wouldn't divert or harm her since she had druid blood.

Ann pulled her hood back, letting her long blonde locks fall loose. "I can't feel Xander's presence...weird. That's never happened before." She reached out with her mind once again, using the lines of energy within the earth and the water to find her brother's mind. Yet no presence came to her beyond the vibrations from the mist and the hot, churning energy of the land.

If someone had already killed him, he'd be gone for a few moments until he revived again. But she knew his connection to her had somehow been blocked so she couldn't sense him.

She'd been dreading the day the past would catch up with them for over five years.

The fog swirled around them, hanging in the air like a heavy cloak. As she stared at the mist, faces appeared with glowing eyes. They had frightened her as a child, but she knew now they were just Asrai. A water fae who lived within the mist—one of the few benevolent Magickind within the five lands. They were just curious and meant no harm.

A female figure made of light jumped into the boat and stared at her, unblinking.

Ed tensed, almost dropping the paddle as his eyes flashed emerald. He let out a low growl.

"It's alright," Ann told him. Though, in reality, she didn't know whether she was saying it for his benefit or the Asrai's.

Ann held out her hand to the creature as her father had taught her. The figure hesitated for a moment, then touched Ann's fingers. The Asrai's touch felt cool and wet, but she didn't sense any danger from it.

"Welcome back, archdruid. You have been gone too long," a gentle voice carried on the wind.

Ann flinched and drew her hand back.

Ed dropped the paddle and reached out for her. "What's wrong?"

The glowing figure of the Asrai melted away as he moved.

"What did it do? Did it hurt you?" His eyes flared with emerald light once again. She guessed it must be a sign of the beast, of some new ability.

Ann shook her head and wiped her fingers against the hard leather of her trousers. "Nothing. It didn't hurt me."

Ed frowned at her. "Then why did you react like that?"

"It's nothing." She raised her hand, calling on the water element. Water magic felt cold, calm and serene. Unlike the raw heat and energy of her fire magic. The cool energy rippled against her fingers as she urged it on. The boat shook for a moment, then moved faster, almost knocking Ed off his seat.

Ann couldn't believe the Asrai had called her that. Darius had been the archdruid. She didn't answer to that title, she wouldn't.

"Sage will know what to do," Ed said, changing the subject. He knew when she didn't want to talk about something.

Ann scowled at the mention of Sage. They had never gotten along well, even when her father had been alive. Sage had been one of his advisers, and a strong, gifted woman within the druid order. "I have no doubt about that, but I do doubt I'll like her suggestions."

"You should listen to her. She's…" Ed rubbed his chin, searching for the right word. "Truthful."

"When have you ever known Sage to be truthful? She only shares things when she feels like it." That was just one of the things Ann disliked about Sage. The old woman marched to her own tune and thought she was above everyone.

"She still has a wealth of knowledge. If anyone can help, it's her."

"Yes, but she will expect something in return." Ann folded her arms, trying not to think of Xander and what might be happening to him.

Ed didn't reply and just continued rowing. The water barely rippled from the movement. The lake looked like a mirror, and their reflections stared back at them.

Ann glared at her own reflection. She hadn't aged much since the night her parents had been killed. Sometimes she didn't recognise herself either. Now, she wasn't sure who she was.

"Will you stay here?" she asked. "After we've seen Sage, I mean."

Ed shook his head. "No, my place is with you."

Ann looked away, feeling something tug at her heart. "You haven't been my bodyguard for a long time now. You don't have to stay with me."

"You don't trust me anymore." She didn't have to look at him to hear the hurt in his voice.

"Yes, I do." She trusted him more than anyone. It didn't matter what he'd become. *Ed had been with her every day since her parents died, up until Orla had taken him away.* "I…you don't have to stay with me out of duty. You need to find out what happened to you. I won't blame you if you want to save yourself for once."

She didn't want him to leave, but she couldn't help but feel guilty. He'd never have changed if it weren't for her.

Ed put the oars down before reaching out and taking her hand. "I'm not leaving you. Not ever. You're the most…I'm not staying out of duty."

Ann shook her head. "People close to me get hurt, you know that."

"Orla can torture me, change me into a beast, or even kill me. But my place is by your side. Always. I stay because I *want* to, not because I have to."

She squeezed his hand, then pulled back. Glancing up at the heavy fog, she muttered the words needed to reveal the opening to Trin. The mist parted like curtains, revealing a small wooden dock on the edge of the tiny green island. A tower loomed at the peak of a green tor, a causeway leading up to it. Giant rocks surrounded the island, serving as a natural barrier that protected it from the waves and elements.

Trin looked just as she remembered it. In a way, it felt like coming home.

Ed drew up alongside the dock and helped her out of the boat. He raised his hand and the reeds unravelled, dispersing back beneath the misty water.

Ann sighed as she stared at the great stone tower. She'd spent months here as a child, learning from the greatest minds in the five lands when all the races had been at peace. This was all that remained of her druid heritage.

Ann took a deep breath and marched along the causeway. She thought about casting a circle and transporting herself up to the tower but decided the walk would help clear her head before confronting Sage. The wind whipped against her, carrying with it the scent of apples.

Once at the top, Ann pulled the heavy doors open. They groaned in protest. Inside, a rainbow of coloured light from stained-glass windows covered the stone floor. Each window depicted battles and major events in druid history, including an image of Ann's namesake,

Rhiannon the Great—one of the very first female archdruids.

A woman in a blue robe stood before the altar that was used for worship.

As their footfalls stopped, Sage turned around. Her long red hair fell past her shoulders and had long streaks of grey in it. Her green eyes held decades of wisdom. "Welcome home, Rhiannon." She came over and took Ann's hands, then kissed her on each cheek.

Ann winced at the use of her full name. "Sage." She gave her a polite nod, relieved when the other druid didn't try to embrace her.

Ed fell to one knee, kissing the hand of the chief druid.

Sage's eyes narrowed. "You've changed, my boy." She cupped his face. "What have they done to you?"

"That's one of the reasons we've come here," Ann said. "But Orla has Xander now."

CHAPTER 6

Sage led them to another chamber containing three wooden chairs

stuffed with cushions, a small fireplace, and a diamond-paned

window. The oak floor looked freshly cleaned, and the smell of

apples from the island's orchard filled the room. Ed smiled at the

familiarity, Trin had been the only real home he'd had growing up.

The druids had welcomed him as an orphan and taught him the ways of their lore. *Darius must have seen something special in him to make him one of the Black Guard, but Ed hadn't been able to save him.*

His smile faded as he felt the tension coming from Ann. She and Sage clashed often, and he suspected Ann blamed Sage for not being able to save her parents.

Ed wanted to ask Sage dozens of questions, but Xander's disappearance trumped everything. His answers would have to wait until later.

As they settled, Sage brought in a tray of tea, pouring it as Ed and Ann explained what had happened. Sage listened in silence as they told their tale.

"We have to find Xander," Ann finished. "Orla hasn't had him long. She might—"

"No. Our first priority is your safety," Sage insisted as she leaned back in her chair. "You can't go running off looking for more Gliss."

"Are you saying we should do nothing?" Ann shot to her feet, her blue eyes flashing. The air around them crackled with power. Ed noticed sparks of fire flaring in the air. This always happened when she felt strong emotions.

Ed felt something clawing at the edge of his mind. Whatever it was, it felt excited by her anger. He guessed it was the beast, or whatever now possessed his body. He gritted his teeth as he tried to push it away. The presence only grew stronger.

"I'm sorry, but yes. Xander is gone." Sage sipped her tea and then set the cup back down. "You should stay here on the island where you'll be safe."

"Xander and I are bound by our blood—we can't die. I can't just leave him whilst Orla tries to torture whatever she wants out of him."

The presence within Ed's mind became stronger, itching to get out. He had no idea what it wanted. The very idea of another being inside him terrified him.

"Xander will lead them straight to you. I can't have that. You must—"

Ann swept her arm across the table in frustration, knocking the cups and pot of tea to the floor. The china shattered, the hot liquid steaming as it covered the flagstones. "I will never give up on him. He's my brother, he's the only family I have left."

"If Orla finds you, she finds the key to the power she craves. If she gets it, she'll plunge the lands into blackness."

"I was an idiot to think you might be able to help. I mean, you let my parents—" As she broke off, Ann's hands clenched into fists and fire burst up from within the empty hearth.

Ed turned his attention to the flames. Somehow, they soothed the raging beast inside him. He took a few deep breaths, and the presence of the beast lessened.

"I couldn't protect them, but I *can* protect the last of the archdruid's bloodline."

Ann stormed out without saying another word.

"Ann?" Ed made a move to go after her.

"Let her go. You know how she is. She still lets emotion blind her even after all her training."

"Can you blame her?" Ed felt a pang of guilt. Neither he nor the rest of the Black had been able to save them as they had sworn to do. He pushed those memories away. No sense in dwelling on a past that couldn't be changed.

Sage raised her hand. The broken crockery vanished, replaced by a new set. "I love Xander, too, but if she goes in to save him, she'll fall right into Orla's hands. That's the one thing we've tried to prevent from happening all these years."

"This is all my fault. I led the Gliss right to them, I failed in my duty, again. I should have—" Ed shook his head. "I don't know what's happened to me." He touched the druid's hand. "What am I? I can't remember any of it. One moment, Ann and I were talking, the next, three months have gone by, and I'm a beast." He gripped her hand. "Please, help me. I can't protect her this way." He paused. "What did Ceara do to me? Why did you send us to see her that night?"

"Ceara wanted to talk to you. She called me in thought, not Flora, which surprised me. You know we never got along," Sage told him. "I was sceptical at first. I knew she wasn't trustworthy after everything she'd done, but she sounded sincere. All I did was pass on the message."

Sage closed her eyes, brow creased. Ed felt her power wash over him as she scanned him with her mind. The beast's presence flared to life again. It clawed at him, trying to force its way out.

"I need to know how to change back. I need to be myself again." He released her hand and drew away from her. His own hands clenched into fists as he fought to push the other presence away.

Sage shook her head. "This is not something that can be changed. I always knew there was something special about you. Now it has emerged." She rose and touched his face. "I don't think this is a curse. This is what you are. Embrace it."

Ed pushed back from the table. Anger heated his blood, and his claws flashed as he gripped the table's edge. "How can you expect me to accept this?" he growled. "I'm one of the Black, not *this*." He couldn't believe Sage wouldn't help him. Not only was she skilled, but she'd also been like another mother to him growing up.

"I'll do what I can, but this seems to be a part of your very being. There may be no reversing that."

"I can't be around Ann if I stay this way. I can't control myself around her. If I hurt her—" He sighed. "I don't want to be this…thing. It's not natural. I've never met any Magickind like this. Orla must've done something to change me into a demon."

"If you can learn to control it, you'll be better than any of the Black at keeping her safe. Besides, there are many different Magickind on Erthea, including those outside the five lands."

Ed shook his head. "I can't live like this. I won't, not if I'm a danger to those I care about."

"Rhiannon is who you care about most, isn't she?"

"I'd never cross that line." He looked away. Many people thought he and Ann were a couple over the years, but there had never been anything romantic between them.

"Perhaps, but it may not be so easy for you to ignore your feelings," Sage said, turning toward the door. "I'll prepare a circle and cast a spell to attempt to remove the presence within you. But are you sure this is what you want? It seems such a waste to throw it away. It's a chance to be stronger and more powerful than you've ever been."

"I'm sure."

Ed went in search of Ann, and instead found Flora Valeran, her aunt.

"Flo." He rushed over and hugged her.

"Ah, it's good to see you, my boy." She returned his embrace and ruffled his hair. "You're looking skinny. We'll have to do something about that."

Ed smiled and hugged her again. It felt good to see the woman who'd taken him in and raised him as her own. He couldn't remember anything about his own mother, or if he even had one. But it'd never mattered. Flo had treated him like her own son along with the other fosterling she'd taken in. "I missed you." He kissed her cheek. "Have you seen Ann?"

"Yes, she's…upset. I told her to cool off." Her smile faded. "It seems I've lost another member of my family."

"Xander isn't lost. I promised Ann I'd find a way to save him, and I intend to," Ed said. "I'm…something happened to me…" His voice trailed off. How could he tell her he'd been changed into a beast? What would she think of him?

"I know. Sage has dreams, and she told me you'd changed. She thinks it's a good thing."

"Only Sage could see this as a good thing." He scowled. "But she's going to reverse it." One way or another, he would get rid of the thing that possessed his body. Despite what Sage said, he doubted this beast was natural. How could it be?

"You're still you, my boy. No matter what you might turn into." Flo reached up and touched his cheek. "You'll always be you."

"I won't let it win," he growled. "I'll find a way to undo this."

"How do you know the beast wasn't already part of you?"

Ed frowned. "How can you say that?"

"There are tales of beasts coming to Asral from as far East as

Lulrien. Ann found you on this very shore with no idea how you came to be here."

He shook his head. "I can't stay this way." He'd travelled all over the five lands, both with Ann and as a member of the Black. He had never encountered any beasts like the one he turned into.

"You don't remember much about where you came from before you landed here," Flo remarked. "I have a feeling this creature is the key to your missing past."

"I'll see you later." Ed gave her one last embrace, then headed outside.

The cool air hit Ed's face as he headed back down the tor. He breathed in the scent of salt and sweet apples. Being back here felt soothing and calmed his inner beast. He tried to ignore its presence and reached out with his mind, relieved his senses still seemed to be working. He felt Ann's presence close by. They had always been able to sense each other, although other people found it strange. Having such a close relationship with his best friend made other women uncomfortable as well.

Ed headed away from the door and through a thicket of oak trees until he reached the orchard. The branches twisted and bowed. The apples and oranges were like tiny works of art dotting the horizon.

He found Ann sitting under an old tree whose branches were gnarled with age. Its fruits long since dead. They'd played here as children. Some of Ed's best memories took place here and were with her and his foster brother, Jax.

Ann didn't look up as he moved over to her.

"I'm sorry about Sage."

She snorted. "I shouldn't expect anything less from her." She picked up a leaf and tossed it away. It sparked with power, hovering in the air for a moment before falling to the ground.

Ed knelt and put his hands on her knees. "We'll get him back. One way or another."

"Don't make promises you can't keep." She pushed her hair off her face. "I won't give up on him, ever. There might be a way for me to find him using a spell my father taught me."

Darius hadn't just been the archdruid—he'd learnt things no druid would. He'd pushed magic to its limits in his lust for power. Even the druid order had been wary of him.

"Ann—"

"Orla can't track me here, so I can use all the magic I like. It's a linking spell. I'll be able to sense Xander with it."

"It sounds risky." Ed settled down beside her. He knew her magic went far beyond that of a normal druid. Ann had gone through training most of the other druids couldn't survive. Darius had wanted her to be as strong as she could be. So, he'd trained her in combat and all forms of magic.

"Come with me then. I need someone in case something goes wrong. Will you?"

"Of course, but first I have to get Sage to get me back to my usual self." He lay back on the grass.

Ann laid down next him. "Once we have Xander back, I'm going to find a way to stop Orla. I'm done hiding," she said. "You don't need fixing. If this is the way you are now, I don't care. You're my best friend. I don't want to lose you again."

He squeezed her hand. "You'll never lose me. Always and forever, remember?" He smiled at the memory of their childhood.

She laughed and rested her head against his shoulder. "Right."

Ed went through the usual cleansing rites and dressed in a pair of trousers but remained naked from the waist up. His heart thudded in his ears. Nerves didn't sit well with him—they never had. He fought anything that gave him fear. He splashed cold water on his face and caught the scent of jasmine—Ann's scent. Strange he could feel her presence so easily now, even more so than before he'd been changed.

She came into the room, dressed in her usual leather trousers and black tunic. "I came to wish you good luck."

His fists clenched. The scent of her seemed intoxicating. He wanted to drag her into his arms and…he banished the thought.

"Are you okay?" She touched his shoulder.

Ed took a deep breath and moved away from her. The beast clawed at his mind, excited, eager to get out. "Yes…just a little nervous."

"You? Nervous?" She laughed. "You never get nervous."

"Hey, that's not true. I was terrified the first time I went to meet your father and be introduced to the rest of the Black."

"Yeah, right." She nudged him. "Good luck. Let me know if Sage's horns finally appear."

"Sage doesn't have horns." He chuckled.

"So you say." Ann wrapped her arms around him.

Ed sighed. He loved the feel of her there but having her this close made him want her more. He pulled away. "Don't start your spell without me, alright?"

As much as he trusted her abilities, he didn't want her going into danger without making sure she had a way back. Not that she needed him to keep her safe. Although he'd been assigned to her back in the days of the Black, she'd never needed anyone to protect her. They'd always been partners, even if they'd had to keep their partnership a secret for most of their lives.

"Yes, sir." Ann gave him a mock salute, but her grin faded. "Be careful. Maybe you should let me perform the spell. I'm a lot stronger than Sage. I'm surprised you turned to her instead of me."

Ed shook his head. "I know you are, but Sage has more experience with this kind of thing." In truth, he didn't want to put her at risk. He had no idea what the spell would do or how the beast might react to it. It was better to keep Ann away. He turned, trying to ignore the urge to pull her back into his arms. "I'd better go."

"Wait, let me scan you first." She touched his arm. "If we can figure out what Orla did to you, maybe you won't have to go through the cleansing rites." She scrambled up into a sitting position.

Ed sighed, but nodded as he sat up. Ann placed her hands on the sides of his head. He closed his eyes and felt her there inside his mind. Her presence wasn't unwelcome. It felt familiar and strangely comforting. Her power rippled through his body, but to his surprise, it didn't set the beast on edge as he thought it would.

After a few moments, Ann pulled away, and Ed opened his eyes again. "What did you feel?" he asked. "Is it a curse? Did you feel the dark magic Orla used on me?" He hoped Orla hadn't somehow forced a demon inside his body. But what other explanation was there?

Ann shook her head. "No, I didn't sense any dark magic within you. Maybe this beast is part of you—you *have* always been different. You can withstand my fire, for one thing."

Ed scowled at her. Why did everyone keep saying that? "I'm not a beast. This thing inside me isn't natural, nor is it part of me."

"How do you know that? Jax is a shifter. Maybe you're some kind of shifter too. If I go deeper into your mind, I'm sure I can recover your memories to figure out what Orla did to you."

"I can't wait that long. I need this thing out of me."

"Whatever happens, your beast side doesn't matter to me. You know that, don't you?"

Ed looked away. That meant more than anything. "Right."

"Listen, I…I couldn't bear if I lost you again. You're the one constant I have in my life." She touched his shoulder, then left.

Ed let out a breath, wondering what was wrong with him. Ann had been one of his closest friends since childhood. He'd never let himself think of her as anything else, yet everything in him wanted her.

Must be the beast, he told himself. *I'll be rid of it soon enough. This madness will pass, and I'll be myself again.*

Ed found Sage waiting for him by the chalice well where the spring's sacred water flowed.. The water was said to possess the power to cleanse away even the darkest of magic. He prayed it would be enough to destroy the beast inside him.

"Ready to begin?" Sage scooped water from the well up in a large silver chalice. She moved over to where the water trickled down from the spring above.

"More than ready. Let's get started." Ed stared at the spring. The water was so pure no one ever went in there other than during magical rites. It smelt of honeysuckle, rich and sweet. Strange he'd never noticed it. He didn't know if it was because of his heightened

senses or because he'd never needed its power before. Part of him

wished Ann were there, but she needed her strength for the linking

spell she planned to use to find Xander.

"You realise it may not work?" she added. "If not, you will have

to learn to control the beast."

"Magic can be reversed. Just do it." He gritted his teeth. The beast

growled at the edge of his mind, and words whispered through him.

He couldn't make sense of them or the feelings the beast projected.

No matter. The beast was just a strange, unwanted thing Orla had

somehow forced inside him. He wouldn't consider the possibility of

being stuck with it.

"This will hurt," Sage warned, sliding down into the pool. "You

need to prepare yourself."

Ed climbed in after her. "I can handle pain." Becoming one of the

Black required gruelling training, including withstanding torture. He'd

endure everything necessary to be normal again. If he couldn't rid

himself of the beast, he might have to leave Ann. That he couldn't

bear thinking about.

Sage chanted words of power in the ancient druid tongue and

making a sign over his forehead. Ed recognised some of the words about casting evil out and cleansing the soul. His body jerked, and his eyes glowed bright emerald, reflecting back at him in the pool. His fangs elongated as the beast emerged.

Don't fight it, Sage told him, chanting louder.

His fists clenched, his claws digging into his palms so hard blood seeped out.

Light washed over him, enveloping his entire body as energy surged through every fibre of his being. It felt exhilarating at first, but he doubled over as pain tore through him, feeling as though his body was being ripped from the inside out.

He clutched his stomach, feeling blood pour from his eyes as his vision blurred red, and the world around him started to darken.

CHAPTER 7

Ann hurried out of the pool. She'd sensed the power in the air and felt something was wrong. Edward lay face down as Sage continued to chant. Her heart skipped a beat when she caught sight of him. What had that silly old bat done now?

"By the spirits, what have you done?" Ann demanded.

"Stay back," Sage warned. "The spell isn't yet complete."

"You'll kill him if you don't stop," she hissed. She sent her mind forth, scanning his body with her senses. To her relief, she felt him breathing. *Edward, are you alright?*

But he didn't respond to her mental call.

"I told him this might happen. I need to be sure I get all of the dark magic out of him." Sage raised her hands and started chanting once again. The air hummed with power.

"He doesn't have dark magic inside of him. You said yourself this beast could very well be part of him, and I believe that. I didn't sense a demon inside him, so I doubt Orla managed to possess him." Ann made a move to climb down into the pool, but a flash of light repelled her. She gasped, surprised the power would repel her. Static sizzled against her skin, making the hair on her arms stand on end. Sage might be one of the oldest surviving druids left, but Ann and this island were connected.

Damn it, she needed to get him out of there. She reached for her power and fire crackled between her fingertips. She wouldn't let anything happen to Edward, especially not now she'd just got him back. But when she raised her hand to release her power, she hesitated. Deep down, she knew she couldn't interfere, or she would put Ed at risk.

Sage continued chanting as lightning flashed overhead. Thunder rolled in the distance, crashing hard like waves against rocks.

When the static finally faded, Ann jumped into the pool, grabbing hold of Ed's arms and pulling him onto the stone ledge. His eyes were still closed, and his body unmoving. *Damn, why didn't I stop him?*

Sage got out of the pool, knelt and touched Ed's forehead. "It didn't work. I still sense the beast inside him." She rose. "I told him it was part of him."

"Why my father had you as his adviser, I'll never understand," Ann growled. "You could have killed him! Are you never going to stop putting people's lives at unnecessary risk?"

Sage scoffed. "He's a beast now. It would take a lot more than that to kill him." She heated the air around her to dry her robe. "Besides, he insisted I cast the cleansing rite. I had to be sure whether the beast was natural or not." She frowned at Ann. "Perhaps you should have done it and start acting like the true arch—"

"Don't you dare question me on how I use my powers." Her eyes flashed with golden light as power rose from deep inside her.

"Good, start acting like the archdruid, Rhiannon. You can't ignore what you are forever."

Ann shook her head as Sage walked away. The old bat was too reckless for her own good. She had no idea what Flo saw in her, either.

Light flashed as she transported them to Edward's room. She used magic to dry him off and laid him on the bed. The room looked just as she remembered, most of it being taken up with a small four-poster bed covered in heavy blue linen. The only other furniture in the room was a small chest of drawers, a table and two chairs. Ed had never been one for keepsakes growing up. The only things he had were a pile of old books, some old clothes and a collection of knives.

"You better not leave me again, you big lug." Ann lay down beside him, resting her head against his shoulder. She couldn't bear the thought of losing him again.

She didn't bother lighting any candles. Pale light filtered in through the diamond-paned windows, bathing the room in a white glow.

Ed's chest rose and fell. This was the first time she'd seen him at peace since he'd come back. His sleep had been uneasy and fitful before. As she watched him, her mind wandered to Xander. He, Ed, and Flo were the only family she had left. She would not lose any of them.

She stayed there until it was almost time for the full moon, and for her to begin her own spell.

"Rest up," she told Ed. "I'll check on you later."

She left his room, leaving the tower's prying eyes behind as she headed down the tor and settled on a spot close to the beach. She had fished here with Ed and Xander as children. Waves crashing against this shore echoed in the distance. Ann breathed in the heady scent of salt as she drew a circle and runes within the sand. She hadn't used magic like this for a long time.

Ann said the words of power, feeling magic rise from deep inside her. She knew Ed wanted to be there with her, but she couldn't drag him into this, nor could she afford to wait any longer. Xander needed her.

Around her, the world became a riot of colour as energy rose up from deep within Erthea. Greens, golds, reds, and pinks filled the air around her. The world's lifeblood flowed in and out of her. It felt good to connect to the earth lines like this again; she rarely did it nowadays for fear someone would sense her power. All druids had a connection to the earth, but Ann's ran much deeper.

The power pulsing around her body felt pure, untouched, uncorrupted. She raised her hand, reciting the familiar words of a spell she'd learnt long ago, and gasped as energy jolted through her. Darkness surrounded her when she opened her eyes, breathing hard. Shackles were wrapped around her wrists and ankles, holding her body upright. Her limbs felt like heavy weights trying to drag the rest of her body down.

Bright orange light stung her eyes, making them water. Ann blinked several times in an attempt to get her vision to adjust to the glare, yet even her eyelids felt heavy and painful.

It had worked. She and Xander were now connected, and she could see through his eyes.

Xander? Xander, are you alright?

Ann? His voice sounded distant, weak.

It's okay, little brother. I'm here now. She scanned the room, almost gagging at the stench of urine and waste.

A torch flickered in the corner, casting a haze that sent shadows dancing around the tiny cell. A door sat on the other side of the room, closed and no doubt locked.

I'm here, Ann said. *Listen to me, I'm going to get you out of here.* She moved his hands, and the shackles rattled. She tried summoning power, but nothing happened. No doubt Xander's powers had been rendered useless. She tried to channel her own power through their now linked minds. Nothing.

Xander, listen to me. We don't have much time. You need to help me find you. Show me what you saw.

In response, Xander's head lolled forward. He had only been gone two days—how was he already this weak?

Focus, Xander! she said, louder this time. *Show me where they took you.*

Xander shook his head as if trying to clear it. *I didn't see much. They knocked me out, and when I woke up, I was in a dark room.*

Show me. Maybe I can spot a clue as to where they're holding you. Ann needed anything that might show her where the Gliss had taken him. Sage's warnings didn't matter; she wouldn't leave her little brother here to be killed over and over again.

I'll try.

Ann let his memory drag her in. She stood inside the warehouse again, seeing herself and Ed fight off the Gliss.

She spotted movement.

In the memory, Xander turned, raising his makeshift staff weapon. Something hit him over the back of the head. He dropped, and the Gliss grabbed him, dragging him away as his vision started to blur.

When Xander opened his eyes again, he found himself chained up inside a windowless room. Was this the first time he'd woken up? His memories blurred together, so it was hard to tell.

"Hello, Xander. It's good to see you again." A raven-haired woman with blue eyes grinned down at him.

"Orla," Xander breathed.

"That's impressive magic that kept you cloaked. It's taken me years to find you." She ran a finger down his cheek. Xander flinched at her touch. "I thought you'd be happy to see me, after all, we were family once."

"Family, ha! You were my father's whore. Nothing more."

Ann felt a burst of pride but winced as Orla slapped Xander across the face. "I am—*was* his true love."

He laughed. "I'm sure a lot of women thought that." He gave her a hard look. "Urien died the night he killed our parents. If you've spent all these years trying to find him, you've wasted your time."

"Did he now? I don't believe you. I haven't been able to find either his body or his soul. Why is that?" Orla gave him a questioning look.

Ann looked around the room, trying to find any sort of clue that would tell her where her brother was being held but found nothing.

"I don't know," Xander replied. "Urien is gone. I can't believe you've wasted all these years trying to get him back."

The memory faded as the cell door creaked open. In walked Orla, wearing her usual black leather bodice and a black silk skirt that billowed around her legs. She pulled out one of her knives, a three-pointed star that could be used to inflict bodily harm and channel the power of the user and ran her fingers along the blade.

Ann winced at the sight of the Fomorian demon. How she wished she'd never set foot in that bunker. She should have known all along it had been a trap. If they had never captured Edward, they never would have been able to take Xander.

Ann, you need to go, Xander said.

No, I haven't found anything to show me where you are yet! Ann wouldn't just leave, not before she found a clue. Besides, she needed to get back at the Gliss for taking Ed away from her.

Ann, please go. You know I'll never tell her anything.

Ann wished she could believe that, but even the strongest person eventually broke under the torture of the Gliss.

Ask her why she thinks she can bring Urien back, she said.

"Why do you think you can bring him back? Our father destroyed him—him and his soul."

"We both know that's a lie. Darius may have banished Urien's soul, but he didn't destroy it," Orla hissed. "He sent it away, and those blasted druids took his body. I know he's still out there somewhere. You will help me find him." She gripped Xander's throat, and shockwaves reverberated through his body, making him cry out.

Ann screamed inside his mind as the same pain shot through her. Orla touched his head, trying to claw her way into his mind. A smile crept over her face. "Rhiannon."

Xander blinked up at the Gliss. "What are you talking about?" he gasped. "Ann isn't here."

Ann, you need to leave now. Go, in case she senses you.

"Oh, I sense your sister there. If you don't tell me what happened to my son, perhaps I can get her to talk."

Ann gritted Xander's teeth together. She'd fry this murderous bitch. She raised his shackled hand and sent her power flying into his body. Again, no magic came to her, but instead, a violent jolt of energy reverberated through him.

Ann gasped, blood pouring from her nose as she slumped to the ground. She lay there for several moments, breathing hard and gritting her teeth. She'd been so close to Xander. Ann knew she could've used her power after a few more attempts. Xander's may've been bound, but hers wasn't, and she hadn't ended the spell. What had brought her back?

"What happened?" Ed sat beside her, brushing her hair off her face as he cradled her head in his lap. "Good thing I brought you out of it when I did."

"Why would you do that?" she hissed. She made to move away, but the world around her started to tilt. "The spell worked; I was with Xander. You shouldn't have done that. I could've found him." She glared at him.

"Yeah, and you're bleeding." Ed used the edge of the blanket to wipe her face. "You were screaming. You can't expect me to leave you like that. You could have—"

"I can't die, remember?" Ann rubbed her throbbing temples. She pushed his hand away and rolled over onto her side, breathing hard. Her body still reverberated with pain—Xander's pain. Spirits only knew what kind of agony Orla had already put him through.

"One day, the spell your father cast might not work anymore, and you'll stay dead. Even *he* wasn't infallible."

"I was right there." Ann muttered a curse. "If I'd stayed longer, I could've found a clue or something to tell me where they're holding him, but instead..."

"Orla knows you're alive too, doesn't she?" Ed said. "Damn it, Ann. You—"

She forced herself to sit up, and her stomach recoiled. "What would you do if it was your brother? I have to get him back."

"We will, but we can't be reckless about it. How long do you think it will take Orla to realise you're the one she needs?"

"I'm done running. One way or another, I will find a way to stop her." She slumped against him, more wounds appearing over her neck and arms as blackness threatened to drag her under. Blood dripped down her chest, and she winced from the pain. *Now what's happening to me?*

Ed gasped. "How did this happen?"

"The spell must still be linking me to Xander. Never mind me, look out!"

CHAPTER 8

Ed glanced up, spotting pools of inky blackness moving in front of the shadow of the full moon. They were shades, lost souls doomed to wander for eternity that Orla often used to track people. Even they could eventually pass through the protective barriers around the island.

Shit. They found us.

He looked down, seeing more wounds appearing over Ann's body. "Ann!" He shook her shoulder, but she didn't wake.

He muttered a reversal spell and traced a rune on her arm. Nothing happened. Another part of his curse, no doubt—he could no longer wield magic the way he once had.

Frustrated, he picked Ann up as though she weighed nothing at all. *At least the beast is good for something.*

Ed sprinted back to the path that led up the tor, making it halfway before one of the shades came straight toward them.

A burst of blue light shot skywards. Sage stood at the top of the tor, her long robe blowing behind her. "Hurry," she called.

Ed ran, so fast things started to blur past him. Air rushed against his body as he moved faster than he'd ever thought possible. One moment he was on the path holding Ann in his arms, the next, he was at the door of the old tower.

"Get her inside," Sage ordered.

He hurried inside the tower. Flo stood in the doorway, long blonde hair falling over her nightgown. "Follow me." She motioned, gliding down the hall. They passed several suits of armour and colourful tapestries as they moved through endless corridors. It almost felt like a dozen eyes were watching them. Silently judging him and what he was now. Ed shuddered and tried to shake off the feeling.

Ed followed her into Ann's room and laid her on the bed, wincing as he heard the heavy slam of the tower's outer door closing. The room looked as he remembered, with a large four-poster bed and rich dryad oak furniture. A heavy green bedspread covered the bed, marked with runes and druid symbols. Books and crystals lined one wall.

"She cast a spell to link her mind with Xander's," he said. "They somehow became physically linked, too."

"She and Xander are bound by blood, so that doesn't surprise me." Flo touched Ann's forehead. "We have to break the connection, or—"

Sage pushed past them, and Ed caught the flash of a knife as she plunged it into Ann's chest.

Ed gasped and looked away. "Couldn't you have come up with a better way?" he hissed.

"It's the fastest and most effective." Sage yanked the knife back. "In death, the link can no longer exist." She wiped the blood away and sheathed the knife on the belt of her robe. "Besides, she'll be fine."

Ed shook his head. He'd seen both Ann and Xander die several times over the years, but it never got easier. He feared the day the spell failed.

"Foolish girl, what was she—?" Sage said, stopping short as Ed cut her off.

"You can't blame her for wanting to save her brother." Ed crossed his arms and looked down to where Ann remained unmoving. It could be anywhere from minutes up to an hour before she returned from death; he knew that from experience.

Sage's cool eyes narrowed. "You've grown soft over the years."

"And you've lost sight of what's important," he retorted.

"There's nothing more important than keeping the last of the Valeran bloodline alive. Darius was the last true archdruid. Without him, our people are dying out," she said. "I promised I would help keep them safe, just as you swore to protect them from the forces of darkness. Ann may not like my methods, but they have been effective over the years."

"What about Xander? He can't die either. What's to stop Orla from using him to find a way to get the power she craves?"

"Xander is expendable. He isn't the key to getting Orla what she wants, but if Ann confronts Orla—"

"I won't let that happen." His beast problem no longer mattered. Nothing came before his duty, not even his own desperate need to be himself again. "And Xander isn't expendable. He's still a Valeran." He was grateful Ann wasn't awake to hear what Sage had said. She'd be livid.

"He isn't the archdruid. It seems to me you've been too lenient with them over the years," Sage remarked. "Perhaps I'll—"

"Who else could have kept them safe?" Ed demanded. "The other druids are either dead, in hiding, or have been swayed to Orla's side by her claim about Ann killing her parents. No one else could protect them."

"Your feelings for her are a weakness. If you hadn't left them—" Sage snapped.

"*You* are the one who sent us to Ceara, remember? I never fail in my duty."

Sage gritted her teeth. "Your job was to keep Ann and Xander *safe*, not to indulge them by giving in to their every whim."

"They both needed a sense of purpose after their lives were torn away from them. Ann was inconsolable after what happened." Ann and Xander had both struggled to transition into their new lives as fugitives. Whilst Xander drank and tried to commit suicide, Ann had been hell bent on revenge.

"Yes, now Ann acts like a rogue. She is nothing like what her father wanted her to be. She doesn't act like the archdruid even though she was born to be one."

"He would—"

"Enough," Flo said as she brought in a bowl of water. "Arguing about the past won't change it. Let the poor girl rest. Sage, let's go back to bed. I'll leave the water here for Ann to wash in when she wakes." She touched Ed's shoulder and gave it a comforting squeeze. "Stay with her. She'll be weak when she comes around."

"You go. I need to perform a cleansing and make sure none of the wards have been breached," Sage said.

Flo nodded and gave Sage a kiss on the cheek. "Don't stay out there too late."

Flo left, and Ed wondered how such a gentle woman could be with someone like Sage. They were complete opposites.

"Not all the Black are dead," Sage said. "You need to make sure your feelings for Ann don't best you. Your love for her cannot come before duty, and you should know that."

Ed gaped at her. "I'm not…she's my best friend. I'd never let anything get in the way of my duty."

"I sense the beast in you magnifies the emotions you had before. You need to be more careful." She turned and strode from the room.

Ed felt his hands clench into fists, and he had to hold back from hitting the wall. Normally Sage never bothered him, but now, he understood Ann's dislike of her.

Ann gasped, her chest heaving as she opened her eyes and took a deep breath.

Ah, thank the spirits.

Some of his anger dissipated as he sat down and touched her hand. "What happened to casting the spell with me there?"

"That bitch stabbed me, didn't she?" Ann's eyes flashed.

His lips quivered as he bit back a smile. "How do you know it wasn't me?"

"Because you value certain body parts that I'd cut off if you ever did stab me." She sat up, scowling at the hole and blood covering her tunic. "You were out cold—I had to cast a spell once the moon came up." She sat up, pulling a sheet over herself. "It worked. I spoke to Xander–Orla knew I was there."

Ed opened his mouth to tell her how stupid it had been to cast the spell, but he didn't. He couldn't say he wouldn't have done the same thing for her. "What did she do?"

Ann glanced down at her arms. The marks had already faded. "She knows Urien isn't dead. She'll torture Xander until she finds what she's looking for." She shivered and hugged herself. "But Xander doesn't know what happened…I have to get back to him. Orla has probably already figured out he can't die." She rose and almost fell over.

"But first you need rest. You haven't used that much power for a while and being killed always weakens you for a couple of hours."

Ann shook her head. "I couldn't see where he was. If I have to search every Gliss compound in all five lands, I will."

He caught hold of her. "Rest, Ann. We'll plan our next move in the morning. Get some sleep." Ed stroked her cheek, then left.

He slumped onto his own bed, staring at the ceiling. How could he be there for Ann with this thing that kept clawing at his mind, trying to get out?

He squeezed his eyes shut. If he had to stay this way, so be it. He'd be damned if he'd let anything hurt the person he cared about the most. His thoughts raced from Ann to the beast, then to Sage's comment, *"Not all of the Black are dead."*

How could that be? As far as he knew, Orla and the Gliss had tortured all of the archdruid's bodyguards and eventually killed them, Ed had only escaped because he'd found Ann. He and Jax had managed to get her and Xander to safety, but he had never heard of any of the other Black escaping.

Could some of them have survived? They had been trained warriors, skilled with weapons and magic, a match even for the Gliss. So, it was possible, but he would have known, wouldn't he?

The thoughts faded as sleep dragged him under.

Blackness surrounded him. It was so thick he could almost taste it, feel it wearing down on him. Ed lay curled up on the floor. No light penetrated the gloom. Every bone in his body felt like it had been broken and fused back together again. The floor felt hard, cold, and harsh. Shadows danced around him like a thousand eyes watching, waiting to see what he would do next. He shivered, his body naked and vulnerable. The cold crept into his aching bones, gnawing and stabbing as he turned over onto his back. His body felt like it had been turned inside out. What had they done to him? Where was he?

The beast clawed at his mind. It felt strong, raw, and hungry. It fought for control, and he felt his body changing again. Muscles popped, and bones bent as it took hold. Claws burst through his fingers and fangs ripped through his teeth. Ed tasted coppery blood in his mouth. Despite the agony, he rose to his feet and growled, launching himself at a door as it became visible through the shadows. His claws tore through wood and metal, yet he couldn't get out. Couldn't break through. He pounded, plunging his fists through the wood. The door somehow held firm. Ed had to get out, had to get back to the person he cared about the most. Ann.

A figure emerged out of the shadows; a woman dressed from head to toe in brown leather. She raised a metal rod, and lightning burst from it. Ed doubled over, the pain radiating through his every nerve ending. Voices echoed around him, asking questions he couldn't make out or understand.

He crumpled to the floor, curling up in a foetal position. The stench of urine and filth made him gag, the sound of his own heart pounding like a heavy drum.

Sudden light burned his eyes.

"Let's see how fast you can heal this time," said a female voice, and he heard a snapping whip.

Pain seared through his back as the whip cut deep into his flesh, lash after lash. It felt as if it were tearing into his very soul.

"Ed?"

He bolted upright, sweat seeping down his face and covering his body. Ann sat on the edge of his bed. He noticed the concern on her face and guessed it was still late, judging by the small slivers of light that came through the window. Darkness still hung like a heavy blanket outside. Similar to the darkness he'd seen in his dream.

"What…what you are doing in here?" Ed rasped. He wiped sweat from his forehead and his heart pounded in his ears. The beast's presence clawing at him, eager to get out.

"I heard you shouting. I came to see if you were okay."

Ed wiped his face, turning away from her. "I'm fine. Sorry for waking you." He put his head in his hands and took several deep breaths. He had to stay calm, or the beast would take control of him again, forcing him to change.

When Ann touched his shoulder, Ed flinched. "You remembered something."

He shook his head. "Nothing important. Go back to bed." He moved away from her. The scent of her enticed him and excited the presence in his mind, but also calmed him.

Ann moved closer to him and put her hands on his shoulders. He made a move to push her away, but she only tightened her grip. "What did you see?"

Ed wrapped his arms around his torso, horrified to feel his body shaking. "Please just go," he told her. "I'll be alright."

She sighed. "You really don't like people being there for you, do you?"

"I'm fine." He got up and splashed cold water on his face. "Go back to sleep. I won't disturb you again."

"Come on, Ed, this is me you're talking to. You spent countless nights with me after awful nightmares about when my parents were killed," she said. "Talk to me."

Ed gripped the edge of the sink and sighed. "I've been tortured before. I'll—"

"The mind can only deal with so much."

He looked at her. "How did you get over your nightmares?"

"I learned how to compartmentalise, but it doesn't work so well now. Between losing you and Xander, I struggle."

Ed slumped next to her. "It's just bits and pieces, being locked up and changing. I think they did this to break me." Gliss enjoyed breaking people. They sat and talked for a while.

"You should get some sleep," he said as Ann lay down beside him.

"I'll just stay here. Doubt I'll sleep much either."

"Sage won't like you being in here."

Ann snorted. "I've slept in your room before. It's not like there's anything romantic between us." She snuggled closer to him and rested her head against his chest, slipping one arm around his waist.

Ed lay there for a while, listening to the gentle sound of her breath as sleep took hold of her. He wrapped an arm around her, and all at once the beast settled, becoming a whisper in his mind. Strange how she had such a calming effect on it. He went over her last words in his mind. *It's not like there's anything romantic between us.*

Right, nothing, he reminded himself. *There never could be.*

CHAPTER 9

Xander's head slumped forward. Every bone and muscle in his body ached. *How long have I been trapped here? Days? Weeks?*

Every second felt like days. They spent hours torturing him by tying him up and flogging him. Or using their rods before a Gliss came in and started stripping away at his mind. Hard to tell which was worse, the physical or mental torture.

Xander had been taught to shield his mind, but it only had a limited effect at keeping Orla and the other Gliss out. There was only so much redirecting his thoughts could do, and it wouldn't protect him forever.

Why I can't be stronger, powerful, like my siblings? Xander raised his head, wishing he could wipe his eyes or touch his pounding head. But they kept him shackled even when they left him to rest.

Rest? He almost laughed. He couldn't rest, not really. His body ached too much, and the constant fear of their return made what sleep he did get fitful and uneasy.

The door creaked open, and Ceara walked in, carrying a tray of food.

Xander looked away as she set the tray down on the floor. She came over and unshackled him, then pulled him up. The only time he had the freedom.

Ceara glanced over at the tray of uneaten food and water she'd left a few hours earlier. He ignored it even though hunger gnawed at him, and his throat felt raw.

"You need to keep up your strength." Ceara sighed.

"Why?" he growled. "You'll only take it away from me again."

"Believe it or not, I'm trying to help you. You wouldn't have this much food if I didn't—"

Xander glared up at her. "Am I supposed to be grateful?" he demanded. "Go away. If you're not here to torture me for information I don't have, get out."

Xander didn't see the point in eating. Too bad they hadn't killed him yet. Death would be a welcome release. One he suspected would allow him to finally contact his sister. Ann had always been able to commune with spirits. He had no idea if it would work, but he knew death was the only chance he had without his powers.

"It's not like you to give up," Ceara remarked.

"I'm not. I know I'll get out of here. When I do, I'll enjoy watching you and that demon bitch burn!"

To his surprise, Ceara didn't strike him as he'd expected her to. Instead, sadness filled her eyes for a moment.

Odd; he hadn't thought her capable of such emotion.

She knelt in front of him. "If you just told us where Urien is, I wouldn't have to keep hurting you."

"Do you say that to all of your prisoners?" Xander retorted. "Get away from me. I'm glad Aunt Flo can't see you now, she'd be disgusted by what you've become." He couldn't keep the contempt out of his voice.

Ceara flinched, and Xander wondered if he'd struck a nerve before dismissing the thought. *She's just acting.*

"How is my mum?" she asked.

"Don't you dare call her that," Xander snarled. "She's not your mother. Your parents never wanted you. They must have seen what a cold-hearted bitch you are." He felt a rush of joy when Ceara looked away. "Flo is the kindest person I know. She loved you, Ed, and Jax like you were her own children. Losing you broke her heart, but you're good at that, aren't you?"

Ceara's dark eyes flashed. "That's not true. I loved—"

"*Loved?* Ha. You're not capable of love. Even Urien didn't love you. You were just a means to an end for him," Xander said. "Like Flo says, you've chosen your path, and where has it led you? You're alone."

Ceara looked away, refusing to meet his gaze. "Does torturing me like this make you happy?"

Xander frowned. In truth, it didn't, but he couldn't help the bitterness he felt toward her. "You bring out the worst in me." He grabbed the cup of water and gulped it down. It felt cold and harsh against his empty stomach and sore throat.

"Why do you want Urien back so much?" he asked, coughing. "I loved you once. What did he ever do for you?"

"He…he accepted me," she said after a few moments. "In a way you and the others never did." She rose and stormed out.

Xander sipped more water, surprised she had left him unbound. She and the other Gliss always shackled him again after they brought him food and water. He looked down at the plate and cup, neither of which would make a useful weapon.

Xander gritted his teeth. Damn it, he needed a quick and easy way to die. Even with his magic bound, Darius' spell would still revive him. He had to reach Ann.

Starving himself to death would be too slow. He needed to die now, so he could find her and warn her to stay away. But without her, what chance of escape did he have?

He tipped the food aside and smashed the plate against the wall. He picked up a shard of it, his hand shaking as he raised it to his throat. He'd have to be quick, or someone might come in and stop him.

Come on, you have to do this. It's the only way to reach Ann.

In one swift move, he sliced his throat. Blood began to pour down his chest as his pulse throbbed. Xander slumped back against the wall and closed his eyes.

Come on, come on, let me die. Spirits, please let this work.

Xander gasped as his body fought to keep him alive, but darkness swallowed him, then an eerie mist surrounded him. He shivered as the cold swept over him.

It worked! He'd recognise the gloom of limbo anywhere. Xander was relieved to feel his pain and exhaustion fade.

Now what? He didn't know much about how spirits in this realm worked. Unlike Ann, who had wandered around it frequently since she had invented a potion to stop her heart and slow the time she revived in.

Xander's mind raced. *Okay, what did Ann tell me about this place? I wish I'd paid more attention! How did she call spirits from here?*

"Ann?" he called. He didn't know what else to try, he couldn't navigate this world like she could. "Ann? Please, if you can hear me, answer me."

He closed his eyes. Spirits could haunt anyone they chose to, but Xander didn't know how to do that yet. Instead, he thought of his sister, reaching out through time and space. *Ann? Where are you?*

Xander waited, but no answer came. The blackness and heavy mist still surrounded him. He muttered a curse, and his mind raced. He knew he didn't have long before his body revived itself.

Ann, he thought again, focusing on her.

Energy jolted through him, a sure sign his body would draw him back any second.

Xander gritted his teeth. "Ann!"

The mist around him drew back, and for a moment, he spotted his sister moving through a glade of trees with Ed at her side.

"Ann?" he called, taking a step forward.

The mist flashed, and another jolt shot through him.

I'm not going back until I talk to her. Xander stepped forward, feeling a ripple of energy forcing him back.

In one swift move, he jumped toward Ann, light flashing around him as he passed through what he guessed to be a portal. For a moment, he stood there.

Ann and Edward were talking, but he couldn't make out their

words. His ears felt as if they were filled up with water.

"Ann?" This time, his voice came out low and garbled as mist flowed around him. He felt like he was trapped underwater, drowning. No one could see or hear him.

He reached out to touch her just as the mist closed around him, pulling him under.

Xander gasped, coughing. His lungs burned for air as he drew in ragged breaths.

Ceara knelt before him, concern etched on her face. "What were you doing, you bloody fool?" she demanded. "You were dead!" She gripped the collar of his ragged shirt and shook him. "If I hadn't revived you—" She frowned, touching the tender spot where he'd sliced his throat. "You're healing. How?"

Xander shoved her hand away and sat up. "Don't touch me."

Damn it, he'd been so close to Ann. If he'd had a few seconds longer, he might have been able to talk to her.

"You were dead," she repeated, spotting the broken shard he'd used earlier. He grabbed it and raised it, only this time he held it to Ceara's throat. To his amazement, she didn't flinch or fight back, she just stared at him. "How are you still alive?"

"I'd be more concerned with your own life right now."

The door banged open as two more Gliss came in.

"What's going on?" the first Gliss demanded. "Why is he unbound?"

As Xander withdrew his hand, ready to defend himself, Ceara punched him in the face. "Stay down," she hissed, rising to her feet.

"Nothing," she told the Gliss. "He didn't want to eat. Leave him to rot for a while. I have other things to take care of."

CHAPTER 10

Ann woke the next morning and headed straight for the records room, where her father had kept maps of all five lands. Despite the ever-changing leadership of territories, she was surprised to find most of the maps were up-to-date. No doubt Sage had purchased current ones for their records and her work with the resistance.

Shelves lined from floor to ceiling covered the room, with books containing everything from the history of the druids to details of harvests. Pale shafts of light crept in through the diamond-paned windows, casting faint white pools over the oak floor. Ann pulled white dust sheets off the shelves in her search for the maps.

She scoured them until she found one that showed the compounds used by the Gliss back in her father's day. They may have been old, but they were still the best lead she had. Ann knew she could reach out to her own network of contacts in the resistance for more current information, but that would take time she didn't have. She had to reach Xander now. Spirits only knew how long he'd survive under the torture of Orla and the Gliss.

"Those will be outdated now." Sage appeared in the doorway. She wore her usual blue robe, and her long hair was swept back in a braid. "You're not going to stop looking for Xander, are you?"

"I'm surprised you'd even ask that." Ann looked up at her and frowned. "You should know I'd never give up on him. Don't bother trying to lecture me about the risks, I'm not leaving him there to suffer."

"Rhiannon, do you remember what I told you the night Edward brought you here, and you told me what you did?"

"You said we had to protect our secret, to make sure Orla and her followers never found out what I did to Urien, or all the lands would fall into darkness again. The lands are falling no matter what. Orla sits in Caselhelm, and her power grows every day."

"Orla is just a puppet with a much more powerful master."

"You mean the Crimson Alliance." She'd always known someone else had helped Orla's power develop but hadn't been able to find much over the years. Most of Magickind worshipped the gods of the Crimson Alliance, but the druids were an exception. They believed in the power of nature and spirits and didn't pray to any deity.

"Imagine what they will do if they have your brother by their side."

"Urien's gone, remember? He's as good as dead, and he will stay that way. Xander isn't powerful enough to be of any use to them, which is why I have to get him back." Ann looked away. She'd never understood why she chose to share her darkest secret with Sage. She'd never even told Xander the full truth of what had really happened to Urien, just that he wouldn't be coming back. Xander never questioned her about it, and just accepted Urien was dead. Perhaps because Sage had understood better than anyone why she'd had to do it. She had to make sure Urien could never hurt anyone else. However, Ann had always known there was a good chance Urien would find his way back, not just because of Orla's efforts.

"You did the right thing that night. You stopped him." Sage gripped her arm. "We made sure his evil could never come back into the world. Everything we've done is to ensure he's never found."

"Sometimes I wonder if it really did any good. Orla still took Caselhelm, and the other lands still fought over it, which led to another war. The other lands are still controlled by the Crimson." She brushed her hair off her face and sighed. "Maybe I just delayed the inevitable. It didn't bring my parents back, did it?" She picked up the map and rolled it up. "Secrets have a way of coming back to haunt you, my father always said that. I'm tired of the secrecy, the hiding. I'll get my brother back, no matter the cost."

"Even if it means plunging the lands into darkness?" Sage moved over to the edge of the table.

Ann shook her head. "I won't let it come to that." She stuffed the map into her pack. "I know you'd have me stay here and act like a good little druid but taking down the Crimson and helping the resistance is too important for me to hide away."

Sage laughed. "I never could make you do anything." She squeezed Ann's shoulder. "After your parents died, I wanted you to remain hidden and safe. But I know what you're doing is important. Be careful, use that sense I know is in there somewhere."

Ann squeezed her hand and walked out of the room to find Flo and Ed waiting for her in the hall.

"I've packed supplies for you," Flo said, pulling Ann into her arms. "I do so wish you'd stay here. Maybe you could find another way to help Xander."

"You know I can't."

"Stubborn, just like your father." Flo squeezed her so hard, Ann flinched. "I worry about you."

"I can take care of myself." Ann pulled on her cloak. "Plus, I have this big lug with me." She gave Ed a quick smile.

"You be careful too, boy." Flo wrapped Ed in a hug and sighed. "You could both be safe here."

"Nowhere is safe for me, Aunt Flora, not really. Orla's forces will never stop hunting me." Ann gave her one last hug and glanced at Ed. "Ready to go?"

He swung his pack over his shoulder. "Where are we going?"

"To the first Gliss compound we can find," Ann said as they headed outside. The wind whipped against them as they made their way down the tor. The mist felt cool against her skin.

"That's the plan? Search every Gliss compound we can find?" Ed remarked. "That sounds like a long shot and a complete waste of time."

"It's our *only* shot." She called up the reed boat as they reached the banks of the dock. "Do you have a better idea?"

"No, but searching Gliss compounds may draw unwanted attention."

"So be it. They took my brother; they'll pay for it." She scrambled into the boat, setting her pack down beside her.

Edward got in after her, and they both waved goodbye to Flo and Sage, who stood watching on the top of the tor.

Part of her felt sad as she watched Trin fade further into the mist with every oar stroke.

Stop being silly, she told herself. *It's not like you're never coming back here.*

"What about you?" Ann asked as Ed rowed back toward the mainland. "What are you going to do about your beast?"

Ed flinched when she said the word 'beast' but shrugged. "I don't know yet. Saving Xander is more important. Once he's safe, I'll find a way to undo the curse they put on me."

"How do you know it's a curse?" Ann said. "How do you know the beast isn't part of you?"

He snorted. "How could it be?"

"Maybe it's linked to your past. You don't remember much about your life before you came to us, but you were ten then."

He shook his head. "I don't dwell on the past. You're my family; whoever came before that doesn't matter."

Somehow, Ann doubted that. He'd often told her he wondered where he'd come from as they grew up, but she decided not to press him

"Sage mentioned some of the Black might have survived," he said, changing the subject. "If they did, I'd like to try and find them.

They'd be a valuable asset to the resistance, and I think they'd follow your orders. After all, you are the archdruid."

"Really? Who?" Ann smiled. She'd been close to many members of the Black. They had been like family to her, and she'd hated losing them after her parents' murder. "It would be good to see them again. I thought only you and Jax managed to escape?" Her smile faded at the memory.

"So did I, but anything's possible. If they're alive, we'll find them."

Once they were back on the mainland, they quickly made their way to the nearest village, Stowcroft. The tiny market town bustled with people, full of different stalls selling everything from plants and herbs to livestock, crystals, and potions. Ann was surprised to see people openly selling magical wares. If anyone was even suspected of using magic, they would be arrested, and most likely put to death. Ann often spent her time helping those accused of using magic to escape to the other lands using her contacts in the resistance. She'd considered asking them for help in the search for Xander, but she didn't want word spreading about Orla having her hands on him.

"We should see about getting some horses," said Ann. "We'll cover a lot more ground than if we're walking. It's less risky if I don't use my magic to transfer us to different places."

They had horses a few months ago but had been forced to flee without them after the Gliss had caught up to them again. Ann hadn't bothered getting any more horses before now. It wasn't unusual for them to change horses when they needed to make quick exits, but now they would need them.

Ann still had some coin left from before her parents' death, and only used what she needed. Life on the run left little time for luxuries. Plus, they couldn't afford to waste precious gold.

Ed nodded. "We'll find some, but we'll need to be extra careful. Let's get something to eat first."

They moved on, cutting their way through the busy streets. People called out to them, trying to entice them with goods, but Ann brushed them off. She always felt a little nervous being around strangers, and it hadn't lessened over the years. To her, everyone could be a potential enemy. She forced herself to stay calm as she and Ed headed inside the local tavern, telling herself she looked nothing like Rhiannon Valeran. Powerful glamour spells disguised their true appearances, so even the Gliss wouldn't recognise her or be able to read her emotions.

The air inside the stuffy tavern stank of sweaty bodies and cheap ale. Dust and grime lined the wooden floor. The tables were scratched and sticky, and some of the stools looked like they were about to fall apart.

Ed ordered them a meal. Ann didn't want to stick around for long, but she trusted Ed's judgement. They often got useful information when they visited taverns. She wished she could summon magic to cleanse the table but knew she couldn't draw any unwanted attention. Despite her glamour, she kept her hood up over her face.

Why can't we just find some horses and get moving? she asked Ed, hoping the beast didn't stop him from hearing her.

Taverns are a hotbed of gossip. If there are any Gliss nearby, we'll hear about them here first, he replied.

Ann sighed and slumped onto a stool. *Make it quick. Every minute we waste —*

I know. Ed headed off to the bar to chat to some of the men there.

She envied how easily he blended in, especially when she was too suspicious to speak to anyone. *Five years on the run must have made me paranoid.*

Instead, she scanned everyone in the bar, spotting a dark-skinned man in the corner. *Is he watching me?* But she pushed the thought away. *Relax,* she told herself. *No one here is going to hurt you.*

She closed her eyes; made sure her mental shields were in place and sent her senses out into the world. The wind outside picked up as she called on the elements to aid in her search. Fire crackled deep within the earth and stone grumbled beneath her feet.

Faces and images flashed through her mind until she spotted a stone temple used by the Gliss. There was usually one in every province. The Gliss actively went after any possible magic users across Caselhelm and its borders. A barrier prevented her from sensing anything inside its walls, and Ann's brow creased as she extended her power, using the elements to probe deeper. The stone walls of the tavern grumbled and moaned as she touched the ancient temple. Old temples often proved to be the best places for Gliss to hold prisoners, since the ancient walls often blocked or contained magic, making it harder for them to escape.

Her mind pushed against the power of the stones, which hummed and groaned with power. Tiny red cracks covered each one, the remnants of wards cast ages ago. Their energy still held strong, preventing her from going inside. They'd be easier to breach if Ann were there in person, but she'd have to make do with trying from a distance for now.

Ann pushed harder, urging the wards to yield to her, but still, they resisted. Red light flashed in front of her eyes. She knew she had to be careful, or she risked alerting any Gliss inside to her presence.

Damn, if only I had a stronger affinity for stone magic.

Her eyes flew open as someone touched her shoulder, but she relaxed again as she met Ed's gaze.

What are you doing? Ed asked. *You know you can't use magic out in the open like this.*

Ann brushed him off. *I was careful.* She gritted her teeth and picked up the drink he had placed in front of her. The buttery beer tasted harsh and warm, but it would have to do for now. She'd try to breach the temple with her mind again later. Ed was right, it was too dangerous to do it here.

"Did you get any horses?" she hissed, knowing she had to revert to talking to avoid looking suspicious.

Ed nodded as he sat down beside her. "Two, at a good price."

Ann arched an eyebrow. "You're too trusting, you didn't even go outside to see them. What if they're old or lame?"

"I saw them on our way in. They're young and strong, they'll get us around." Edward scanned the bar too. Men gathered round the bar, laughing and shouting as they drank their beer as two serving women in dark dresses moved around carrying trays of food.

A dark figure in the corner wearing a black hooded cloak caught her attention. Something about him didn't feel right. But she couldn't make out his face underneath his hood.

Have you spotted that guy in the corner? Ann said. *He keeps watching us.*

You're a beautiful woman even when you're hidden by a glamour—men watch you.

She scowled. *I don't want to be watched. Where is the server? It would have been quicker to have breakfast before we left Trin.*

Relax, would you? He reached over the table and gave her hand a quick squeeze. *You're more nervous than I am.*

I need to get to that temple. We could just buy some bread and eat on the way.

Ed shook his head. *If we stay here long enough, we should be able to find out if the temple is occupied and how many Gliss are in there. They have to eat, so they probably come into the tavern quite regularly.*

They ate their meal in relative silence. Ann grew annoyed at the lack of leads they heard. She noticed that the man in the corner hadn't moved once the entire time they'd been there.

"I'll pay the bill, you can get the horses," Ed said.

Ann headed outside, relieved to be out of there as she breathed in the scent of grass and hay. She spotted the white mare and brown stallion Ed had procured for them. He was right, they weren't bad-looking animals.

The door banged, and the cloaked man appeared behind her.

Turning, she pulled out her knife. "If you think I'm a helpless woman who'd make an easy target, you're dead wrong."

"I'm looking for someone. You wouldn't be Rhiannon Valeran, would you?" His voice sounded rough. She still couldn't make out his face underneath his hood.

Before she could hide her fear, all colour drained from her face. "I don't know that name," she growled.

"Really? Because there's a big reward going to bring her in, dead or alive," he said. "I felt you use magic in there."

Ann grabbed the man by the throat and held her knife to it. "I'd back off if I were you."

The man laughed, revealing the face of a ghost. "You're lucky I spotted you first, Ann."

CHAPTER 11

Ed walked outside to find Ann with a knife to another man's throat. *I can't leave her alone for a minute.*

"What's going on?" he asked. He moved over to Ann's side, feeling the beast stir. "What are you doing to my friend?" Ed's hand went to the knife at his belt. The beast clawed at the cage of his mind, begging to get out. He wouldn't give in to it, wondering why it only seemed to emerge when Ann was in danger. He didn't have time to ponder the thought, as the man's eyes shifted to him.

"Are you one of the Black?"

Ed grabbed the man by the collar of his shirt, yanking him away from Ann and lifting him off his feet. "What do you want? If you're here to make some quick coin, you picked the wrong people to target." He shoved the man away. *Ann, let's move.*

"Brothers and sisters, yours in life and death," the man recited.

Ed froze as the very words he'd used when he had sworn fealty to Darius and taken the vows to become one of the Black echoed through his mind. "How do you know those words?"

The man pulled back his hood. "Because I said them the day I pledged myself to the archdruid," he said. "Don't you recognise me?" He had dark brown skin and even darker eyes. He grinned, showing perfect white teeth that lit up his handsome face. He smelled of leather and the coppery tang of blood, Ed noticed.

"Jax?" he gasped. "Is it really you?"

Jax grinned. "You do know me. It is you under there, isn't it, Ed?" He eyed Edward up and down. "You don't look like you. I'm guessing you're glamoured."

Ed hugged him, clapping him on the back. "By the spirits, I can't believe you're alive!"

Jax slapped him on the shoulder. "Brother, I knew you'd be the one taking care of the—"

"Julius Jaxson, how in the name of the spirits are you still alive?" Ann demanded, now unfrozen from the shock of seeing him. She didn't let her guard down, catching hold of him and pressing her knife to his throat again for a second in warning before lowering it again.

"It is you, Ann." Jax laughed, hugging her. "You're—"

"Answer the question, Jax." She pulled away from him.

"Ann, we should get moving. Jax—" Ed said, stepping between them

"He's not coming with us," Ann snapped. *Just because he's one of the Black doesn't mean we should trust him. We haven't seen him in months. Not since he disappeared on his last mission.*

"He's right, we should move," Jax said. "I came to warn you about the bounty."

Ann's eyes narrowed. "How did you even know I was alive?"

"I'm still one of the Black. I can sense the pull of your power. Like it or not, you and the Black are still connected, archdruid."

She flinched. "Don't call me that, especially out in the open like this," she hissed. "Spirits, you were stupid to confront us out here. Don't you have any sense at all?"

Ed, I don't want him with us. She folded her arms. *He could be a spy.*

Read his thoughts to find out, Ed suggested. He wished he could do it himself, but thanks to the beast, it was no longer an option.

I can't do it here!

Then I guess we'll have to take him with us. Ed suppressed a smile. He knew he should be wary of Jax, too, but part of him couldn't help but be thrilled to see his brother again.

"Let's go, Jax." Ed grabbed the brown stallion, and the horse snorted, scraping its hooves on the ground anxiously.

"What's wrong with your horse?" Jax said.

"No idea." He'd been around horses most of his life and hadn't had one react to him this way before. The horse backed away from him, getting more agitated.

Did the horse sense the beast within him? If so, how could he convince it he meant no harm?

Stop that, he said. *I won't hurt you. Please.*

Damn, he needed to get rid of this beast. It caused him nothing but endless problems. Even horses couldn't be around him now without being reviled by him.

The horse snorted again.

Ed's fists clenched, and he growled, his eyes flashing emerald. To his amazement, the horse settled down.

"What just happened?" Jax stared at him wide-eyed. "What did you do?"

Ed shrugged. "Don't know." He climbed up into the saddle, watching as Ann climbed up onto her mare, scowling at him before taking off. *Bugger, a pissed off Valeran is no fun!*

When they were a good distance away from the town, Ann stopped in some nearby woods. The smell of pinecones and wet grass filled the air.

Ed wasn't surprised. No doubt she would want to interrogate Jax.

"Jax, get down here so I can read your thoughts," Ed said, jumping down from his horse. The animal tossed its head from side to side, still uneasy.

"What?" Jax frowned.

"Ann's safety comes first, and I don't trust anyone. I'm sorry, brother, but I have to do it."

What are you doing? Ann asked mentally, giving him a pointed look. *You can't read people's thoughts. Even if you try, Jax might sense the beast in you. He's half shifter himself, remember?*

I have to try. It's the first thing one of the Black Guard would do to a potential enemy, he replied.

You're not one of the Black anymore, she pointed out. *You're different now.*

I'll always be one. I took a vow. Ed fought off a wave of irritation; he didn't need to be reminded of just how different he was.

But what if your power doesn't work? Ann frowned at him. *I don't think you should tell Jax about your beast side—not until we know more about it.*

Do it with me then. We can link minds.

She shook her head at him. *I don't want to take that risk either. You don't know if we can do it anymore.*

"I'll do it," Ann said aloud. "I won't take any chances."

Jax climbed down off his own horse. "I served Darius, and now I'll serve you." He ran a hand over his bald head. "We've known each other a long time, Ann. I know I've been gone a while. I got into some trouble whilst watching Orla for you. Long story which I'll tell you about later. Don't you trust me anymore?"

Ann crossed her arms. "I can't afford to."

He fell to one knee. "I've been working as a bounty hunter since I escaped a Gliss temple a few weeks after the revolution. Those bitches tortured the living daylights out of me, but I lived, and I made some coin, that's all. I'd never hurt you; being a Black is who I am."

"We'll see." Ann placed her hand on his forehead.

Ed stepped back, hating feeling useless. He and Ann had worked together side-by-side for years, but what use would he be to her now, without magic? Would they even have a partnership anymore?

Ann's forehead creased, and after several moments she stared down at Jax. "I'm sorry for what Orla did to you." She pulled back and looked at Ed. "He's telling the truth, as far as I can tell."

But that doesn't mean he's not a threat, she added. *Orla has tried tricking us before.*

Without another word, she swung herself back in the saddle.

"I don't blame her for being wary," Jax remarked to Ed. "But you know I'd never do anything to harm you. We're family, remember?"

Ed heard Jax's heartbeat pick up, realising perhaps he wasn't as powerless as he imagined. "Why have you come looking for us now?" Ed asked him. "It's been five years. We lost track of you after we fled from Larenth after the revolution. I know you went in search of surviving Black. Did you find any?"

"It's a long story. Let's move."

As they made their way to the Gliss temple, Ed gave Jax a brief version of what had happened after the night of the revolution and what they had been doing since then. Including their work in the ongoing fight against Orla and the Crimson Alliance and Xander's capture.

"Darius cast a spell so none of his children can die?" Jax said. "How? I mean, I know he was powerful, but...I always wondered how Xander came back to life after we dragged their bodies out of the palace. What happened to that bastard Urien?

"That's a long story, and to be honest I don't know all of it myself," Ed replied. "Ann did something to him…" He shrugged. "Anyway, we have to find Xander. Whatever happens, Orla can't know Urien's alive or she'll try and bring him back."

"She seems…different." Jax inclined his head toward Ann, who rode ahead of them.

"She is. She's a different person now."

"Orla knows she's alive. She won't stop hunting for her," Jax said. "I meant what I said. I won't walk away from my duty. I can't believe I hadn't found you guys long before now."

Ed didn't mention about his beast. He didn't know how Jax would react to it.

The temple loomed as they approached the top of a cliffside. Its rectangular stone construction an ugly duckling among the trees.

Ann dismounted, pulling Ed aside as they approached. "Are you sure you're okay to go in there?" she whispered.

"Of course. Just because I can't use magic doesn't mean I'm useless," he replied. He still had strength and speed on his side. Even if magic had left him.

I never said you were. Maybe you should start testing your new abilities.

He frowned. *New abilities?*

The beast in you seems pretty strong and powerful. See what else it can do.

What if it takes me over? It's taking all my strength just to keep it at bay.

Instead of fighting, start trying to control it. If it's part of you now...

It's not a permanent part, he growled. *I will get rid of this thing.*

I'm just saying, make use of it, accept it.

I won't accept it. How can you ask me that? Ed demanded. *Do you think I want to stay this way?*

I don't care if you go all beastie, you're still you, Ann said. *If you stay this way, it won't change the way I see you.*

"Let's go and search for Gliss," she said. *Oh, and don't get overprotective.*

Can't help it, given your annoying habit of getting into trouble.

Hey, I resent that! How many times have I got us into trouble? She crossed her arms.

Give me a few hours, I'll write a list. He chuckled.

Ann gave him a shove and shook her head. "Jax, why don't you go and scour the other side of the temple?"

Jax frowned. "Is that a subtle way of trying to get rid of me?"

Ed bit back a laugh. Jax knew them better than he thought.

"No." Ann crossed her arms. "I need to know how many Gliss there are and what potential threats might be inside."

Jax took off his cloak. His body blurred as he shifted into a large crow with glossy black feathers. He squawked and took off into the air.

Ann frowned at the building, all cold hard stone and no windows, just a few columns and a set of double doors.

"I can't get through the wards," she said. "My power won't penetrate them. Maybe you could use your beast?"

Ed frowned. "What?"

"I know you hate what you are now, but maybe you should use it to your advantage."

"Ann, we've had this conversation." Ed's eyes flashed as the beast clawed at his mind. It wanted out of the mental prison he'd put it into. "You have no idea what it's like when I let it out. I feel like it takes over. It feels like I'm going to lose myself." His hands clenched. "Every time it takes hold, I have to fight harder to win control."

Ann reached up and touched his cheek. "You just have to try."

"What if I can't? What if I lose myself?" He had no idea what would happen if the beast took permanent hold. What would it do? Would he become a prisoner inside his own body?

"You won't. I won't let that happen. You trust me, don't you?"

"That's a stupid question. You know I do."

"Then trust yourself. You helped me learn to control my magic. Let me do the same for you."

Part of him wanted to protest, to tell her he needed to be rid of the thing, not learning to control it, but he wouldn't give up, not if it helped them find Xander.

"Fine, I'll try," Ed said after a few moments. "I've no idea where to start, though"

"You have senses. What do you hear? Start with that."

Ed winced as he let his hearing sharpen again. Leaves and twigs sounded like tiny explosions as they rustled and cracked. Ann's heartbeat sounded like a hammer against an anvil.

"There's so much." He clutched his head as his temples throbbed.

"I know. When I first learned to listen to people's thoughts, everything seemed loud and overwhelming. Try to focus on one thing."

He closed his eyes. The beast clawed at his mind, growling—on edge and eager to get out.

Ann's fingers felt warm against his skin as she took hold of his hand. "Focus."

The beast settled, and a sense of calmness washed over him. *Are you using magic?*

No, you big lug. I'm holding your hand.

The world around him became quieter, though he could still hear the thump of her heartbeat.

"Listen, what do you hear inside the temple?" Ann asked. "Do you hear people?"

Ed's brow creased as he focused on the building. The wind echoed through the empty corridors. The air smelt damp, of decay and rotting carcasses. Dead rats, he guessed.

"It's empty." Ed opened his eyes. "I don't hear any heartbeats."

A loud squawk made Ed wince as Jax flew over to them. He shifted back into human form. "No sign of any Gliss." He glanced at their entwined hands. "Are—"

Ed quickly pulled away. No doubt Jax would start asking unwanted questions.

"I still want to check it out. They could have moved Xander."
Ann said. The three of them approached the entrance of the temple.
Sure enough, there were no guards around.

Ed, what do you hear? Ann asked. *Maybe you will make out more now
we're closer to the building.*

He frowned. Everything once again had become loud and harder
to make out. He wanted to reach out and grab her hand again but
didn't. If he became stuck with this beast, he'd have to learn to
manage it alone.

"Hey, are you two talking in thought?" Jax glanced between them.
"I used to hate you doing that."

Ann snorted. "I have to keep him in line."

Jax stifled a snigger, and Ed rolled his eyes.

Come on, focus. What do you hear? she asked.

I think you nag me more since I got back. Ed sighed and closed his eyes.

He heard the scurrying of animals, the thud of their tiny hearts,
and the steady drip of water. It made him clutch his head.

"You okay, Rohn?" Jax asked.

Ann clutched Ed's hand again. "Focus," she whispered. "You can
do this."

He concentrated, trying to ignore the sweet scent of her, then took a deep breath. "There's no one here. It's abandoned."

Jax frowned. "How do you know that?"

"That's a long story," Ed said.

"It doesn't mean they aren't still close by." Ann let go of his hand and disappeared inside.

"Wait, it doesn't mean there aren't any traps either!" Ed hurried in after her.

"I already scanned the area, stop being such a big baby," she said.

"So, are you two finally a couple now?" Jax asked.

Both Ann and Ed froze and turned to stare at him. "We're not a couple," they said in unison.

"Why would you even think that?" Ann asked.

Jax shrugged. "Maybe because of the way you act around each other."

Ann rolled her eyes. "He's practically my brother. I don't know why anyone would think we're a couple. That would be too strange." She disappeared down the corridor, conjuring a fireball that floated above their heads to light their way.

Ed couldn't help but feel a stab of disappointment at her words.

151

"Still haven't told her how you feel, have you?" Jax hissed, shaking his head. "Jeez, some things never change."

"Oh, believe me, they've changed, but she's right. I am—" Ed stopped short as he felt the crackle of energy in the air. "Ann!" He raced down the corridor to find another room with a glowing field of energy blocking his way and Ann trapped inside.

CHAPTER 12

Ann spun around as light flashed. Damn it, she'd scanned for any potential threats. The elements hadn't warned her of anything. The fireball she'd conjured earlier snuffed out, plunging the room into blackness. "Bugger!" she muttered, glancing around the darkened room. Its stone walls glittered with runes that flared with light as their power came to life.

Ed appeared outside the trap. "Why didn't—?"

"Again with the protectiveness." She put her hands on her hips, then sighed. "I didn't sense anything. The power in the runes only shows up when someone activates them."

Ed pushed against the barrier until light flashed and he muttered an oath. "There must be a crystal or something around here somewhere. Start checking the walls."

Ann ran her hands down the first wall, then raised one, calling her fire. "Or maybe I can blast my way out."

Nothing happened

"Oh, no!" she groaned.

"What?" Ed asked, glancing around as if expecting a threat to pop out.

"I have no power. Damn it, that means the entire room is sealed." Such rooms had been designed by the Gliss to weaken prisoners so they became much easier to torture and break. The runes could only be deactivated from outside.

Ed thrashed against the barrier, then came crashing to the ground as he was hit by a blast of glowing blue light.

"Ed and I can get you out," Jax said, appearing in the doorway.

"Or maybe I can shift and—"

Ann shook her head. "No, it's safer if neither of you comes in here. Just look around and see if you can find a way for me to get out. There should be a switch or a crystal to unseal the room."

Jax glanced at Ed as he scrambled up. "You were always better a spell crafter than me."

Ed started tracing runes on the wall, but to Ann's dismay, there was no sign of magic forming.

Damn, I feared that might happen.

"Why's it not working?" Jax asked, frowning. "What's wrong with your magic, brother?"

Ann caught a flash of emerald in Ed's eyes and called out to him. "Ed, focus. You can control this." She gripped the edges of the doorframe, wincing as energy burned her hands.

"Control what?" Jax glanced between them. "What's going on, Ed?"

"Nothing." Ed paced up and down, his body tight with tension.

"Jax, look around. There must be another way out of here," Ann said.

"Would one of you please tell me what's going on?" Jax

demanded, turning to Edward. "Why are you acting so strange?"

"That's a long story," Ann told Jax. "Please just go and look for a way to get me out of here."

Jax muttered something under his breath and walked off.

Ed shook his head. "This thing inside me is going to drive me mad! It's worse whenever you're in danger."

"I'm not in danger, look at me. I'm right here." She placed her hand on the energy barrier.

He stared at her for a few seconds, then put his hand against hers.

"See, control." She grinned. "It's alright, we'll figure this thing out together. You controlled it when we were together outside, you can do it again."

"You won't be alright. You've been trapped, and—"

"I can't die, remember? Now just relax and go and help Jax."

He nodded and disappeared.

Ann let out a breath. Great, her best friend was on the verge of losing control again, and she was stuck in a magicless room. *Okay, got to figure out a way to get out of here. Fast.*

Hours seemed to drag by as the three of them tested different ways to get through the trap. Eventually, Ann slumped onto the floor, feeling herself growing weak. Her eyelids grew heavy as fatigue washed over her, and she closed her eyes and rested her head against the back wall. The coldness from the floor seeped up through her legs as the discomfort she felt faded away.

The empty room around her blurred and the darkness seemed to swallow her whole.

"Rhiannon!" someone called her name, but the voice sounded far away.

Ann blinked, finding herself standing in her father's chamber. Her mother lay a few feet down the hall, her eyes glassy. *Oh no, not this! Anything but this!*

"Rhiannon," the voice called again, weaker this time.

She crawled over to where her father lay. He'd been stabbed numerous times, and Ann had no idea how he was still alive. "Papa," she gasped, trying to draw magic that wouldn't come.

"Listen, I don't have long!" Her father's chest heaved with every breath he took. "You must be strong; remember everything I've taught you…Live for me."

She rested her head against his shoulder and let the tears flow. She felt his life slip away. Around her lay the bodies of her mother, Xander, their guards, and fallen Gliss.

Ann knew she would die here too—she'd used too much power to stop Urien and didn't have the strength to fight anymore—but she didn't fear it. In the distance, she heard shouts and screams. No doubt Orla's forces would be on their way to finish her off. At least she would be with her family again.

Ann gasped as she woke. Her head pounded, and her limbs felt stiff from disuse. She tried to move and couldn't. "Ed? Jax?" she rasped. The memory faded as she blinked. She didn't know why her mind had chosen to go back to that particular moment.

"I'm here," Jax called from outside the doorway. "But we've got another problem. Rohn is changing into something, and I think I'm about to become his next meal."

Ann groaned as she forced her body to move and started crawling across the cold stone floor. "What's he doing?" She fought to stay awake but being cut off from her magic, and her connection to the earth, exhausted her.

"He's got glowing eyes, claws, and fangs!" Jax yelled. "What should I do? I don't want to kill him!"

Movement blurred as Ed flew at Jax, slamming him against the wall.

Ann continued to make her tediously slow journey across the floor, yet the doorway seemed miles away. "Ed, stop, this isn't you!" she said, her voice coming out stronger than she'd expected.

To her amazement, Ed stopped, glancing at her. He looked more beastlike now than he had before, his face distorted.

"Put Jax down. Now!" she snapped.

He let go of Jax, who grunted and crawled away. "This is incredible! He's—"

"Jax!"

"Oh, right. I still haven't found a way out, but the moon is up, it must be affecting him."

Ann finally reached the halfway point. "Ed, you need to focus. Remember…"

"What are you doing?" Jax asked.

"Trying to get him back in control, so the beast retreats."

"Given how it moves, maybe we should use the beast to get you out."

Ed started pacing again, growling as he clutched his head.

"Ed, Ann's stuck in that room." Jax pointed to her. "Look how weak she is."

Edward threw himself at the barrier so hard that a blast of energy sent him flying.

"Hurry, Ed. She'll die if we don't get her out."

"I can't…" Ann pointed out.

"Play along, pass out or something. The more agitated he becomes, the harder he'll try to get you out."

Ann slumped down and closed her eyes. She heard another roar of fury as Ed continued to thrash against the barrier. *I hope you know what you're doing, Jax!*

Seconds later, Ed broke into the room.

He lifted her into his arms as if she weighed nothing. They moved so fast her head spun. "Jax!" she cried as they reappeared in the hallway. She was defenceless; her magic wouldn't come back straight away; she'd need time to recover.

"Stay calm, I don't *think* he'll hurt you," Jax said.

Ed stared at her, running a hand over her face.

"That makes me feel so much better," Ann muttered.

"I'm okay, put me down," she told Ed.

Ed sank to his knees, dropping her to clutch his own head. She rolled onto the floor with a grunt, her already weakened limbs protesting with every movement.

"What's wrong with him?" said Jax.

"I think he's trying to change back, but I don't know. He only reappeared a couple of days ago, so I don't know what the beast does," she told him. "He vanished for three months."

"Orla tried turning all of us after your father died. It looks like it must've worked." He held out a hand and helped her up. "They couldn't change me since I'm already a shifter."

Ann touched Ed's face. "It's okay, come back to me now. Everything is alright."

Edward gasped as his eyes returned to their normal shade of brown and his claws and fangs retracted, and then slumped back against the wall, unconscious.

Ann let out a breath she hadn't known she'd been holding.

"Spirits, I need a drink." Jax fumbled in his pack, pulled out a metal flask and gulped down its contents. He held it out to Ann.

"I don't think that'll make me feel any better, but thanks." She pushed the flask away.

"Why didn't you tell me he's been turned?"

"It wasn't my story to tell."

He shot her an annoyed look. "It would have been nice to know my brother might try to eat me. How long has he been like this?"

She shrugged. "No idea. He reappeared two nights ago when Sage sent Xander and I to help him. Gliss followed him, but he doesn't remember what happened" she said. "What did you mean when you said Orla tried to turn you before?"

Jax gulped more booze down before replying, "After the revolution, the Gliss rounded up most of the Black and tortured us. She wanted us to swear fealty to her, to become her followers. She tried to break us with the worst torture I've ever seen, but we refused, so she tried experimenting on us instead. She wanted strong, powerful warriors, more powerful than the Gliss or the Black." He glanced at Ed. "I guess she succeeded, but the beasts I saw back then didn't look like him."

"Sage thinks the beast is part of him, and I'm beginning to think so too. Flo used to tell us stories of beast men who came over the border through the veil, so I guess it's possible." She cradled Ed's head in her lap. "Why does he only seem to respond to me, though?"

Jax snorted. "I thought that'd be obvious. He's been besotted with you for years."

Ann shook her head. "No, there's nothing romantic between us. There never has been."

"Yeah, you keep telling yourself that. Why else do you think the beast is so protective of you?"

"Maybe because *he's* always been protective of me." She sighed. "We can't be stuck here for the night. I have to find Xander." She made a move to leave, but her legs wobbled, her head spinning with dizziness.

Jax caught hold of her waist. "Yeah, but we're resting here. Neither you nor Rohn is fit to travel."

"What happened to the rest of the Black?" she asked. "Were they turned too?"

Jax shook his head. "I tricked a Gliss into letting me out, but as far as I know, all the others died."

Ann let out a breath. "So much senseless murder." She settled down next to Edward. "It's good to be among family again."

Now I just need Xander back.

CHAPTER 13

Xander blinked, surprised to find himself standing in the great hall of the palace in Larenth. It looked as he remembered it. Same floor etched with brown diamond shapes. Same pale walls. Same glittering stained-glass windows depicting the druids at different times in their history. Light shone through them, casting pools of rainbow-coloured light across the floor.

Why am I here? He hadn't set foot in the palace in five years and knew he could never go back there.

At the head of the hall sat a large dais containing a throne made of dryad oak, engraved with symbols of the *triquetra*—the sign of the Three—and the Valeran crest, a white oak tree surrounded by three stars.

Two smaller seats sat next to it: one for Deanna, one for Rhiannon, Darius' heir.

Xander's heart twisted as he stared at his father's seat of power. Would it even still be there? Would Orla occupy it now?

Ceara appeared beside him. She wore a long grey dress instead of her usual leathers. "Hello, you." She gave him a quick kiss.

He stared at her. "What are you doing?"

Her dark eyes widened. "What do you mean?" she laughed.

"I mean you kissing me. Why are we here?"

"Did you drink too much last night? My brothers are a bad influence." She took his hand. "You live here, I can't believe you forgot! What did Ed and Jax give you?" She tugged at his hand.

Xander pulled his hand away, gripping her shoulders. "You're doing this, aren't you?"

"Doing what?" Ceara demanded. "Xander!"

"Let me out. I can't show you; I don't know."

"Xander, I don't understand. You're scaring me." Ceara clung to him, her body trembling.

He wanted to fight it, to fight her. He needed to get out of whatever illusion this must be, but having her there in his arms felt so real.

"I don't know what happened to you," Ceara murmured. "But I'm here, I'm real. I won't let you go."

Xander held onto her and sighed, though his mind protested.

Ceara's hand flared with light as she reached up and caressed his cheek. Her magic felt warm and familiar. Comforting.

He relaxed and returned her embrace. "I'm sorry. I just…I guess I drank too much. I don't remember."

Ceara snorted. "I heard you were on the floor last night. I told you not to drink with my brothers because they'll drink you under the table."

They moved through the great hall hand-in-hand. Being with her like this felt familiar, right, even.

"I can't believe your father managed to bring about a treaty to unite Caselhelm, Asral, and Vala. We'll finally be able to travel freely like we always talked about."

He'd almost forgotten about the treaty; it had happened before…

Before what?

"I've always wanted to explore the other lands further. I hate we're so divided. This is the way forward for all of Magickind."

"We'll have fun. You can sing and study, and I'll be working with the Black." She grinned. "I can't wait."

Xander nodded. Something still didn't feel right, but he couldn't place what. He was at home with the woman he loved.

She kissed him and turned away. "I'll see you later. I have training with my brothers." She left him.

As Xander stood there, hours seemed to pass. After a while, he went in search of Ceara and headed for her chamber. He opened the door to see her in bed, half-naked on top of someone.

Urien. His heart stopped as his brother smiled over at him.

"Xander!" Ceara gasped, scrambling away from Urien. "This isn't…I didn't—"

Urien grinned as he climbed off the bed. "Couldn't keep her satisfied, could you, brother?"

Xander lunged at him.

Xander groaned, forcing the memory away as he stared up at Orla.

Orla laughed. "See, I can walk through your mind and make you see anything I want."

He felt tears sting his eyes, and his heart ached like it had been broken in two, but he gritted his teeth, blinking several times. "Doesn't matter. I don't know what good that memory serves anyway. Ceara means nothing to me." He glared over at Ceara, who stood in the corner. Her magic had done that to him.

"To prove to you that no matter how hard you resist, I can make you see whatever I choose to," Orla said. "Show me where my son is."

Light blinded him as Orla's magic dragged him back under. Pain tore through his head, feeling as though his skull would explode.

Xander found himself in darkness this time. He groaned, trying to remember where he was. Pale slivers of moonlight shone through the familiar window. He lay in bed, alone. Warm. Safe.

He called forth fire, and the lamp beside him flared to life, bathing the room in an orange glow. It chased away the shadows that had been surrounding him. He spotted the familiar, never-diminishing pile of clothes in one corner. His books, instruments, and scrolls lined the walls. As he climbed out of bed, a scream echoed down the hall.

His heart raced, his feet cold against the wooden floor as he hurried out into the hallway. No guards stood in the hall. Odd, the guards were usually out here day or night.

Xander ran along the hall as he heard another scream. He raced toward the sound, freezing as he saw his sister kneeling on the floor with her arms around their mother. Deanna's eyes were glassy.

"Mama? Mama, no!" He fell to his knees. "What happened? Who did this?"

Ann shook her head. "I don't know. I couldn't get to her in time." Tears rolled down her cheeks as she rose. "I've got to find Papa."

"No!" Xander wailed, reaching for their mother. "She can't die."

"Xander, listen to me. We can't help Mama now, she's gone. I'll find Papa." She gripped his shoulders. "You need to go and find Edward. Don't trust anyone else. Get somewhere safe."

"We can't just leave her here!" he cried.

"We won't. I'll come back for her; I promise." Ann hugged him. Her nightgown was soaked with their mother's blood. "Papa will know what to do, he'll find a way to bring her back."

Xander nodded mutely as Ann hurried away, then clutched his mother's hand. "I'll be back, Mama." He let go of it and walked down the hall. He didn't know where to go, but he had to find Edward. The sound of shouting and something exploding brought him out of his daze.

Papa! Papa is in trouble!

Forgetting all thoughts of finding Edward, he hurried down the corridor. As he ran, he stopped by a window, horrified to see that fire lit up the night. He spotted the Black and the palace guard fighting off a crowd of dark figures and realised the palace was under attack. *Ann's right, must get Papa. No time to find Edward. How did they get in? Did the Black betray us?* His mind raced as he hurried along the hall toward Darius' chamber.

In his hurry, he crashed into someone. "Spirits!" he gasped, heart pounding.

Ceara looked just as alarmed as he felt. "Xander, what are you doing here? You're not supposed to be here!"

His eyes narrowed. "Ceara? I thought you left with Urien?"

"I did, but…Listen to me, you have to go. If Orla's people find you, they'll kill you."

Xander pushed past her. "I should have known you were a traitor."

Ceara grabbed hold of him. "No, you need to go. Please, I don't want you to die."

Xander stared at her. His heart twisted, but he shoved her away. Nothing would stop him from reaching his father, especially if Orla was after him.

As he moved down the hall, another figure appeared. Orla. "Fancy seeing you here," she grinned. "You haven't been easy to find. Unlike Deanna."

Xander raised his hand and drew magic, screaming as he channelled his power outwards. His hand sparked with blue light, and he cried out a death spell, a type of magic he'd never used before.

Orla waved the spell aside as a burst of air made her stagger. "Oh, little Valeran, you always were the weak one," she laughed, throwing something at him.

Xander barely had time to catch a flash of silver before he gasped as something ripped into his stomach. When he looked down, a knife had embedded itself in his abdomen.

"Excuse me, I'm about to witness my son take his rightful place as the next archdruid." Orla turned and hurried away.

"No!" Ceara caught hold of him. "No, this wasn't supposed to happen."

Xander brushed her aside and stumbled down the hallway. Blood seeped down his nightshirt, but he kept moving. He had to reach the chamber, had to find his father.

"Stop, you stupid fool." Ceara reached for him again, but he ignored her. "We've got to go. I'll find you a healer, I promise."

"Let go of me!" he snapped.

"You'll bleed out. You will die if—"

"I don't care. I've got to find Papa." He stumbled again, looking down to see a trail of blood. He felt no pain.

Ceara wrapped an arm around him, supporting his weight. "You have to stop. We have to get out of here."

"So you can drag me off to Urien?" he spat at her.

"No. I didn't come here to watch you die, let me help you."

A wave of dizziness washed over him, and he leaned on her more heavily. "Please, take me to my father. I have to get to him."

Ceara nodded and helped him reach the doors. Inside, Darius was battling Urien, and Ann fought off Orla in one corner. Just as Darius crumpled to the ground, Ann blasted Urien with her fire.

Xander's vision blurred, and he too fell to the floor.

"No, Xander." Ceara's voice became distant.

He pulled the knife out of his stomach and threw it toward Urien in a vain attempt to stop him. Darius lay unmoving, his body burned and bleeding.

"Xander, you can't die!" Ceara cried.

"Ann?" he called for his sister, but it came out in a whisper as blackness took him.

Xander blinked. That had been the first time he'd died, just before Darius' spell brought him back. Strange, he hadn't remembered much about that moment until now.

Orla let out a cry of frustration. "There must be more!" she snapped at Ceara. "Go back into his mind, go deeper."

"I can't. If I do it again, I might damage it," Ceara snapped back.

"What does that matter?" Orla demanded.

"He's no use to us with a broken mind."

Orla stormed out, slamming the cell door behind her.

Ceara came over as blood dripped down Xander's face, coming from his nose and mouth. She grabbed a cloth, wet it using a bucket of water in the corner, and wiped the blood off. "I'm sorry," she whispered. "I had to go deep. It was the only way I could bring the memory to the surface."

Xander blinked up at her. "You...you tried to save me."

She gave him a sad smile. "I never wanted you to die. She promised she wouldn't harm you." She shook her head. "I was stupid to believe her."

Xander's head throbbed as he closed his eyes. He'd always thought Ceara had been the one to stab him. He remembered running into her that night, but everything else had been a blur. "You made me forget," he said as she rubbed the cloth over his face. "Why?"

She shook her head again. "I tried to use my power to heal you, to take your pain away, but it didn't work. You died anyway." She turned away, not meeting his gaze.

He leaned forward, his shackles rattling. "Why would you do that? Why did you care about what happened to me?"

"Because believe it or not, I did love you," she said. "I never wanted you to die."

"If you loved me, why did you sleep with my brother?"

"Because he was…exciting, powerful. So different from you."

"Right. Poor, boring, powerless me." He looked away. "That's exactly what you said the day I found you two together."

"I am…I can't change the past. Urien made me feel special, he didn't fear me being a Gliss."

"Neither did I. I loved you."

Ceara hung her head. "He accepted me, made me feel important. He told me that instead of being an outcast, I could be strong, powerful," she said. "I loved having him look at me like that, making me feel that way."

"You really think he would have given you all that? This is Urien we're talking about."

"He's not a bad man, there's good in him too. I saw a side to him no one else saw." Ceara smiled.

Xander shook his head. "You still love him, don't you?"

"Of course I do. Why else do you think I'd put up with his bitch of a mother?" She reached out to wipe his face again.

"Don't touch me. Just get out."

Pain filled her eyes. "I want Urien back more than anything, but I don't want to see you hurt." She turned and left, closing the cell door behind her and leaving Xander alone with his memories and thoughts of what Orla would do next.

CHAPTER 14

Ed was in a foul mood the next morning when he heard he'd lost control again. In front of Jax, no less. He hadn't wanted Jax to know—he wouldn't understand. Despite the fact Jax was a shifter, Ed knew his beast was nothing like Jax's crow form. Jax's body merely took on another shape. He didn't have to fight another presence for control.

"You didn't do anything bad. Well, there was a moment there when I thought you were going to eat me," Jax added. "But you got Ann out, so that's the important thing."

Ed rested his back against the log next to where they had set up camp outside the old temple. The morning sun rose high in the sky, chasing the night away with its bright rays.

"That's not the point. I could have killed you, damn it! I can't stay here. I need to find a way to control this," he said.

"Are you just gonna leave us? I just found you again, and we took a vow, remember? Brothers in life and death. Besides, you can't leave Ann. She's the only one who seems to get through to you when you're being controlled by that thing. I still can't believe you haven't told her, though." Jax took a bite of the bread he'd toasted over the fire.

"Told her what?"

"You know what, Rohn." Jax crossed his arms. "That you love her."

"Of course I do, she's my oldest friend."

Jax threw his hands in the air. "I give up! You'd refused to tell her five years ago. I don't know why I thought now would be any different."

Ed shook his head and sipped water from a wine sack. "I can't, you know there are rules against that kind of thing. Different races are forbidden to have relationships with each other." He took a bite of his own toast. "People have been killed because of the laws against different Magickind interbreeding."

Jax snorted. "She's never cared what race you are." He broke off another piece of bread and held it over the simmering fire. "Heck, I'm half shifter and half something else that gives me incredible strength. My birth parents obviously never cared about the stupid rules, whoever they were."

"Anyone of mixed race is frowned upon. We're outcasts, remember? Rogues of magic. Our lives are complicated enough as it is." He sighed. "Ann and I are still fugitives. More than one realm has a price on our heads."

"What does that have to do with anything? I still don't understand why you won't tell her how you feel."

"Because I can't cross that line. I can't believe you're still bringing this up after all these years."

Jax grinned. "I'm bringing it up because nothing's changed. You still deny your feelings for her." He took another bite of toast. "So, are you gonna leave?"

Ed shot a worried glance over to where Ann sat studying the map a few feet away from them. To his relief, she hadn't paid attention to their conversation. "No, I can't break my promise to her. I have to help find Xander, but then I have to get this thing out of me." He sighed. "You'll have to take over from me while I do. One of the Black needs to stay with her. I have a feeling things are going to get a lot worse."

"Maybe it calms around her because of your feelings for her."

Ed opened his mouth to protest, but Ann called, "Are you two going to sit gossiping all day, or are we gonna check out more temples?"

They'd scoured three other temples in the past few days. One had been unoccupied, and the other two had been filled with Gliss but offered no sign of Xander. They'd barely escaped from the last one, while Jax fought off Gliss in the entrance, one slipped through. Ed had lost control again and ripped her apart after she tried to grab Ann.

"Let's move." Ed stalked off.

They left the horses behind to rest and graze, while they made their way through the town of Gilley on foot. In the town centre, a crowd of people gathered around a woman tied up to a pyre. She had long red hair, parted at the front by small black horns. Her eyes were a vibrant gold, signifying her Ursaie nature. Ursaie came from outside the five lands. They'd been kept as slaves for thousands of years, forced to suppress their strong magical talents. Most races within the lands despised them, thinking them no more than a scourge on Magickind.

"This woman is accused of using magic against her master," someone announced. "By the laws of Caselhelm, she is hereby sentenced to death."

Ann touched Ed's arm. "We have to do something," she hissed.

"We can't, not without drawing attention to ourselves."

He wanted to help accused magic users as much as she did. But, they usually did so undercover, not out in the open like this.

"Ed, we can't let an innocent person die!" She crossed her arms and raised her chin, giving him a determined look he knew too well. "Bringing freedom to the five lands and liberating magic users for a better future is the very thing we're fighting for."

"How do you know she didn't use magic to do something bad?" Jax asked.

"If she had, there's no doubt the Gliss would have swayed her to their side. Pardoning corrupt magic users is how Orla finds allies," Ann said. "I'll take care of it. Be ready to make a quick escape and waylay any Gliss if they get in the way."

Ann pushed her way through the crowd of onlookers. They were native to Caselhelm and close kin to the druids, but the majority had been enslaved under Orla's rule.

"How do you manage to keep her safe?" Jax said, watching as she moved forward.

"Sometimes I wonder that myself," Ed remarked. *Ann!*

He pushed through the throng of onlookers after her. If she got into danger again, he worried about how his beast would react, he didn't want to risk innocent people getting hurt.

Ann, we can't interfere! If I lose control again…

Don't, she replied.

It's not that simple. Please, let's just make our way to the next temple.

The woman screamed as a guard lit the pyre, and the flames began to lick around her feet. Her golden eyes flashed as she struggled against the bindings holding her to the pyre.

Ann vanished from sight, and Ed muttered an oath as he scanned the crowd for her. The beast in his mind panicked, clawing to get out and take control once again. Cheers rang out as the woman called for help and begged the guards to release her, but Ed still couldn't see Ann anywhere and realised she must have cloaked herself.

"I can't see her, can you?" Jax hissed.

"No, I can't sense her."

Use your beast senses, Jax said mentally.

Ed gaped at his friend. *I don't know how!*

He didn't want to waste time arguing. He had to find Ann before she got herself captured—or worse, exposed them all.

Okay, beast, help me find her! It felt stupid talking to the thing, but what other choice did he have? He didn't want to lose control again, and if working with it proved helpful, he'd do it.

The world around him suddenly became brighter and sharper as he felt the beast at the edge of his mind.

Light flashed, and he spotted Ann kneeling at the edge of the platform, her enchanted cloak hiding her from view. She raised her hand, and the flames snuffed out.

Ann, get away from there! He pushed through the crowd as people started muttering in confusion. "Jax!" He motioned for his brother to follow him.

Ann muttered something, and the pyre crackled, falling forward off the platform.

Two Gliss appeared, knives in hand, and jumped from it.

Ann grabbed the Ursaie's arm, blasted her free, and dragged her away.

Time to go! she called.

Ed ran forward in a blur, knocking the first Gliss to the ground. Inside his mind, the beast roared, trying to break free. As the other Gliss came at him, he blocked her blow and sent her flying with a shove. *I guess this beast might as well be good for something.*

Ann, go! You and the Ursaie get out of here, Jax and I will handle this.

Jax pulled out a staff that had two sharp metal ends, swinging it at the first Gliss, who had pulled herself to her feet and flown at him.

Ed stopped fighting long enough to let the beast have full control, surprised when he remained conscious. His eyes flashed as he heard a whir, and as he ducked, two Mystica knives came at him. They were deadly weapons that could channel dark magic.

He flew at the second Gliss, grabbing her by the throat and lifting her off her feet.

She touched his arm, but strangely, the contact didn't burn him.

"Where is Xander Valeran?" Ed growled.

She laughed. "I'm sure he and his sister will be reunited soon enough."

Ed frowned, gripping her tighter. "What does that mean?"

She laughed again, then pulled out another knife and tried to stab him. Before she could, he snapped her neck.

Around him, people were screaming and flailing around as they scrambled to get away from the Gliss who pursued him, Jax, and Ann.

"Jax, follow me!" he yelled.

CHAPTER 15

When Xander opened his eyes, even his eyelids felt sore. His throat was raw from screaming. His head felt like it had been filled with lead, too heavy for him to even look up. They had moved into a different cell, which he suspected was because Ceara had grown fed up of the stench in the last one. However, this one, with its dark stone walls and thick cloaking of ancient dust, proved no better.

Water dripped from the ceiling, making him shiver. He was chained to another metal chair, which he guessed was the only thing holding his body upright anymore.

The Gliss with long black hair and dark eyes was there again, holding a compress over his eye. She came to tend to him after every round of excruciating torture, whenever Ceara wasn't around. Ceara seemed to have been avoiding him since their last encounter.

He didn't know why they bothered. Why not just leave him this way? Part of him would have welcomed death. If he could escape to limbo again, maybe he could contact his sister. He hadn't given up hope of reaching her yet, and nor would he.

"Can't have me weakening, can you?" Xander murmured.

"Mistress Orla doesn't want you in bad condition," the Gliss replied. She pressed the compress harder against his eye, making him wince. It almost made him miss Ceara; at least she was a bit gentler than her Gliss sisters.

"Haven't you figured out by now that I can't die?"

"Yes, how is that possible?" she asked. "You're the son of the archdruid, but—"

"I don't know." He flinched. "Look, why can't you people just accept I don't know where my brother is? Don't you think I'd have told you by now if I did?" They had wandered through his mind so many times he doubted he had anything else to hide. They knew him, knew his innermost secrets and desires. Especially Ceara. Orla seemed to enjoy making her use her powers on him and read his mind as much as she could. He'd shown them everything they wanted to know, yet still, it wasn't enough. What more could he tell them? He didn't know where Urien was, or what Ann had done to him.

She'd never explained the specifics, and he'd never asked. It didn't matter, the bastard had killed their parents. Xander didn't care what happened to Urien. In truth, he hadn't cared since finding him with Ceara. He accepted Urien was dead, gone along with their parents.

Xander grew weary of the endless beatings, being dumped underwater, and enduring the excruciating torture of their rods, but it was better than when they touched him. The touch of Gliss caused agony and made flesh smoulder when they chose to.

"You still haven't told us where your sister is either," said another voice.

Orla walked into the room as the Gliss left. Her dark eyes held a coldness in them that made Xander wonder what his father had ever seen in her. Darius had loved beautiful women; it had been one of his weaknesses. He'd never been able to stay faithful to anyone, not even his own wife. But he had never been bothered by race. He'd like powerful women, so Xander guessed in that respect Orla fit the bill.

"Even if I knew, I'd never tell you. Ann won't stay in one place. She will keep moving, and you'll never find her." The only things he'd managed to block out so far had been his most recent memories of Ann. Along with the secret of their connections with the resistance. Deep down, he knew Ann was the one they really needed. Only she knew what had happened to Urien.

Orla laughed, the sound low and harsh. "I know your sister better than you think. She tried to save you the night of the revolution. She won't leave you here." She ran a finger down his bruised cheek. "You don't have your father's beauty. Pity, he was such an exquisite man."

"Is that why you helped Urien kill him? Because he chose to marry someone else instead?"

Orla's eyes flashed, and she snorted. "Darius married your mother because her royal blood gave him more power, but I was his first and only true love. I killed him because he was weak in the end. Now I have three lands under my control, and where are his successors? Fleeing from me."

He gave a harsh laugh. "My father never loved you. He never loved anyone except for himself, and perhaps my sister. He loved power above everything else." Orla's eyes flashed, her power simmering in the air.

"You don't control all of the lands, though, do you? Even Caselhelm is divided into different territories now. During my father's rule, it was united, a place of freedom for all races," Xander retorted. "There are still people who oppose you."

"Do you have a death wish, boy?" Orla lifted his chin, forcing him to look at her.

"It doesn't matter how many times you try to kill me, I won't stay dead," he hissed. "I know why you're doing this, but your precious Urien is gone."

"You're lying. My boy isn't dead, and I will find him."

"He's dead. My father killed him."

"Liar!" she snarled. "I know my Urien killed him after I slit your mother's throat and Rhiannon knocked me unconscious. I stabbed you before you had a chance to get into Darius' meeting chamber, so Rhiannon must be the one who did something to Urien."

Xander managed to shake his head slightly. "I don't know, I was dead. I didn't wake up until a few hours later."

"Rhiannon must have told you something. You two were always close, and I am going to find out." Orla grasped the sides of his head again.

Xander squeezed his eyes shut, making sure his mental shield still held. Even if it did him little good, its presence felt comforting. He couldn't let her into his innermost thoughts again, in case she found anything about Ann's whereabouts. No matter how much pain she put him through, he wouldn't. Pain tore through his head, making him feel like his skull would explode, and his brain would burst out.

He tried to move past the pain just as Ann had taught him. She had trained with the Black, learning things he would never have dreamed of, nor wanted to. He wasn't a fighter, but a scholar at heart. One who enjoyed telling tales and hooking up with beautiful women. He had never wanted to be dragged into this mess. Maybe if Darius hadn't turned against the druid order in his lust for power by sleeping with Orla, none of this would have happened.

He clung to his mental shield like a child clutching their favourite blanket.

"Xander, are you even listening to me?" a voice demanded.

He looked up to see one of his tutors glaring down at him. "Can you do anything right, boy?" he hissed. "You're worthless. I'll never make a warrior out of you." He shoved Xander to the ground and pulled out his belt. At the time, he'd thought the beating had been the worst pain in the world.

Xander moved into the yard, where Rhiannon fought with one of the Black Guard.

"There, my girl fights better than most of my men. Why can't you be more like her?" said Darius. He beamed as he went over and embraced Rhiannon. "There's my girl. So strong already."

Xander looked away. He'd always wanted their father's approval. But he'd never resented Darius' love for Ann. She'd always taken care of and comforted him.

Orla laughed. "Yes, Darius could be a bastard, couldn't he?"

Xander blinked. "No…"

"I glimpsed into your mind and saw what you were thinking. I know you still have more to show me, to tell me."

"No!"

She laughed and left the room. He heard the murmur of voices outside.

He had to get out of there, had to reinforce his shield. How could it have weakened?

Xander tugged at his neck restraint and slumped forward so the collar tightened, cutting off his airway. He gasped as his lungs burned for air.

Come on! Let me die. They won't have time to start torturing me again if I'm not here. Xander closed his eyes, letting the blackness of death drag him in.

It felt cold and empty in limbo. He let out a breath, almost feeling safe away from the pain and torture.

"Come on, Ann. I know you can hear me!" he yelled. "Rhiannon!" His voice echoed through the shadows, but there was nothing. Xander paced up and down, wracking his brain for anything of use and cursing the fact he was better with potions.

There must be a way I can get a message to her, but what would I say? Help, come rescue me, I don't know where I am? Come on, think.

You three will forever be bound by blood, his father had said…

"Blood." Xander glanced at his hands, but he wasn't flesh and blood in this world, nor could he move his physical body.

He gasped as he felt a magnetic pull, the signal of his body drawing his spirit back.

"No, I won't go back! I'm not ready!"

He tried to grab something, anything but the misty haze of limbo passed through his fingers.

Light hurt his eyes as Xander awoke to find himself lying on the floor of his cell.

"Little bastard thought he would escape me in death," Orla scoffed. "I'll make him pay tenfold for daring such a thing."

Xander kept his eyes shut and slowed his breathing. His chest ached, and his lungs still burned, but he'd endure it. For a few precious moments, he was free of his bonds.

"At least you broke into his thoughts," said the voice of the Gliss who'd tended to him earlier.

"It's not enough, and it's taken me days to get through. That wretch is stronger than I thought," Orla sighed.

"There's a bounty on Rhiannon and Edward Rohn. Sooner or later, someone will find them."

"We risk people turning on us. Darius and his queen were loved, how do you think people will react when they learn his daughter still lives? They could rise up against us!"

Orla, is that fear I hear in your voice?

"We'll find her, mistress. Soon, all of the lands will—"

"I need my Urien by my side. He's Darius' heir, and he will be the next archdruid."

"Then lure Rhiannon here. Force her out into the open. What about her aunt and the druid Sage? Why not use them?" The other Gliss suggested.

"They're safely hidden away on Trin."

"The Gliss could find it and break through their wards. You know we could."

Xander squeezed his hand, wincing as he forced one of his wounds to reopen. He muttered words of power and let the blood flow.

"Ann?" The room around him faded, and he reappeared inside a field.

"Xander!" Ann stood in front of him. "How?"

"No time. Listen to me, Flo and Sage are in—"

He never got the chance to finish his sentence, as pain dragged him away.

CHAPTER 16

Ann winced, her head pounding like a heavy drum. The room around her looked hazy and distorted. She closed her eyes, trying to remember what had happened. She'd helped that woman get free from the pyre, and they had made a run for it as Gliss chased after them.

They'd made it as far as the woods when the woman had stopped, pretending to be injured. Ann had started to examine her, then everything had gone black. She hadn't even had a chance to react or to even see if she had been close behind them.

Damn it, she must've hit me over the head. Ann rubbed the back of her aching skull and saw she now had a metal band on her wrist. *Great, I've been bound.* She sat up, noticing she'd been dumped in a dank, dirty, windowless cell. The air smelled stale and musty like the room had been locked up for years, but something about the grey stone seemed almost familiar as if she'd been there before.

A torch flickered in the corner, sending shadows dancing across the walls as bursts of orange light chased the gloom. They'd taken her cloak—even though its protective magic wouldn't have been detectable to anyone but her—and no doubt her weapons. *Damn, why did they have to take the cloak? They could have at least left me with that.* The magic would be useless without her own power to supplement it. Still, it had sentimental value and would have kept her warm.

As Ann scrambled up, the room spun. She ignored the sensation, gripping the wall. It felt cold and hard to the touch, and there was no murmur from the stone. She hated feeling so disconnected from the elements, it felt like part of her had died.

There was no sign of Xander anywhere. Bugger, she'd hoped they'd have put them closer together so she could see him and make sure he was okay. Ann thought she'd seen him standing in the woods for a moment. He'd said something about Sage, but she hadn't been able to make out what.

"Orla?" she called. "Come on, I know you're around here somewhere."

The cell door creaked open, and through the shadows, in walked the woman she'd helped, now dressed in a brown leather jumpsuit.

"Argh, I should've known you were a Gliss." Ann crossed her arms.

"It's been a long time, Rhiannon. I must say your true appearance looks much better than your glamour."

Ann's eyes narrowed. "Do I know you?"

"Don't remember me?" The woman smiled and walked into the light, revealing her true appearance. "I didn't think you'd have forgotten me already."

"Ceara? I guess I shouldn't be surprised to see you. You're the one who dragged us into this mess." She crossed her arms. "Damn, I should have seen past your glamour. But how did you see through mine?"

Ceara laughed. "You forget how well I know you. I grew up with you, remember, I know how you work, how you think." She smiled. "I knew you wouldn't be able to resist helping someone in need, especially a slave. You always tried to protect your family's Ursaie slaves from being mistreated."

"Yes, well, my father and I disagreed when it came to slavery." She straightened. "Where's Xander? Take me to him, I want to see him."

"You're in no position to tell me what to do. Besides, Orla will be here soon. We want to know what happened to Urien." Ceara put her hands on her hips. "Why don't you tell me? It will save you a lot of pain."

Ann snorted. "He's dead. Even if he wasn't, he wouldn't come back to you. You were only a means to an end for him. He used you to get what he wanted. What that was, I don't know, but he's not coming back."

Ceara slapped Ann so hard her head snapped back, and bile rose in her throat as the world started spinning again. "I am Urien's true love, and you took him from me!"

Ann stared Ceara down, ignoring her stinging cheek. She wouldn't show any weakness in front of a Gliss. "You've been searching for him for the past five years too? How tragic."

"We already know Xander can't die, and from the way you jumped in to save me when I was burning on that pyre, you can't either," Ceara snapped. "Now that we have you, it's only a matter of time before we bring Urien back from wherever you sent him. I know he's alive; he'd never leave me."

"Right, you keep telling yourself that."

Ceara's fists clenched. She had always had a quick temper. "Urien will come back and take his rightful place as archdruid, and Orla will be merciless. She'll enjoy—"

Ann snorted as she cut Ceara off. "Urien is gone. You and his mother both need to accept that."

Ceara laughed. "Enjoy these last few moments without pain because Orla *will* force you to tell her what you did to Urien."

"Even if Urien came back, he wouldn't be interested in you. He only ever cared about meeting his own selfish needs. I guess he took after our father in that respect."

"He loves me. I still speak with him; all he wants is for us to be together again. You'll pay for what you did to him." She grabbed hold of Ann again, her hands flaring with bright blue light as she gripped the sides of Ann's head.

Pain exploded inside Ann's skull, a burst of light whirling in front of her eyes as her vision blurred. She doubled over, clutching her head as Ceara drew back. Images blurred through her mind so fast it felt like lightning was dancing around her skull, whizzing back and forth, and she collapsed to her knees.

Ceara banged the door shut behind her as she left the room.

Ann rested her head back against the wall, the chill from the stone seeping into her skull. It felt almost soothing. She couldn't make out anything but a kaleidoscope of colours and a cacophony of light and sound.

She guessed Ceara had used her magic to weaken her, perhaps as payback for her words. It was hard to believe they had once been good friends. Though not as close to her as Edward, Ceara had been the only other girl around Ann's age. She had always wanted to join the Black, like her brothers. Ann had shared that dream, despite its ridiculousness given she was the future archdruid. She'd never have imagined their paths taking the drastic turn that they had.

Ann fumbled with the bracelet, but no matter how hard she tried, it wouldn't come loose. Her vision cleared enough for her to look down at the plain metal band etched with glowing runes that blocked magic.

She knew they'd torture her, but no matter what they did, she'd never reveal what she'd done to Urien. She'd wiped those memories from her mind long ago, knowing that Orla might one day capture her and try to pry the information from her.

Her secret would be safe, but she still needed to get to Xander and find a way out of there.

Ann rose and ran her hands along the walls, searching for any possible weaknesses. As she did, she realised that she recognised this place because she and Xander had played in the unlocked cells as children. Darius had been livid when he found out they'd been down here, that was the first time she'd seen the darker side of him.

There were back in the palace in Larenth—her childhood home.

I should have known Orla would bring me back here. What did Ceara mean when she said she still speaks to Urien? That's not possible.

Ann paced the length of the room, trying to remember how she and Xander had played there. But the cells had been unlocked. They had run in and out of there with ease. The door creaked open and in walked Orla herself. "Hello, Rhiannon. You've grown up."

"Save the chitchat. I've nothing to say to you, demon," she snarled. "I don't know where Urien is, and even if I did, I'd never tell you."

Orla laughed. "Strong, defiant. I see so much of Darius in you."

"Well, the man you murdered *was* my father." Ann's hands clenched into fists as she reached for her magic and felt it pulsing through her veins, just below the surface. *Damn the bracelet!*

"Murdered is such an ugly word. Darius proved unable to lead the lands as archdruid. I did the people a favour."

"Really? Because last time I checked, the lands are still in chaos and you're on the verge of a war with more than one territory. At least the lands were at peace during my father's rule," Ann snapped, shaking her head. "Why am I even arguing with you? Where's Xander? I want to see him." Talking was a waste of time. She needed to get to Xander, figure a way out of there. Spirits only knew what condition he'd be in after being tortured for so long.

"You are in no position to be making demands." Orla turned to the door and motioned for someone. Two Gliss came in, both dressed in their usual brown leathers. One had long black hair and icy blue eyes, and the other had green eyes.

Ann punched the dark-haired one in the face and kicked the other one in the stomach, causing her to double over.

Ceara came in, grabbing Ann's arm.

Ann grunted and gritted her teeth as the heat of Ceara's touch seared her skin. She lunged at Ceara, who blocked her blow and yanked her arms behind her, shackling them in place.

Three more Gliss came in to subdue her as they dragged her from the cell.

They strapped Ann to a metal chair and brought in a machine connected to wires that had to have been left over from before the dark times, back when they had technology for everything. Erthea had been a very different world then. This room was larger and much brighter than the cell she'd been dumped in earlier. It had whitewashed walls, and crystal torches lined one side of the room, bathing it in an eerie red glow. She shifted her wrists to find the metal from the shackles digging into her flesh so she couldn't move.

"Using tech on me. Jeez, are your usual torture measures not good enough?" Ann gave a harsh laugh.

"I know you better than you think, Rhiannon. You were always the favoured one. Darius shared many of his secrets with you. He would have taught you how to shield your mind," Orla said as she walked into the chamber. "With this, I can break down that shield and find out where you put my son. Darius bound you three together in immortality because he feared Urien would kill you, which means Urien is still out there."

Ceara jabbed the wires into Ann's head and arms, making her wince as tiny needles pierced her skin.

Orla disappeared from the room, and Ceara looked down at Ann. "You wouldn't have to go through this if you'd tell us where Urien is."

"I don't know. You're wasting time trying to find answers I don't have," she hissed. "Urien *will* turn on you, you're just too stupid to realise it."

Ceara snorted. "I'll enjoy every minute I watch you suffer. You'll never know—"

"Save it. Urien is gone, and he's never coming back. I made sure of that."

Before Ceara could reply, Orla came back in and turned on the machine.

Ann cried out as the machine sent shockwaves through her skull and down her spine. She gritted her teeth, trying to remember her training and willing herself to fight through the pain and not let it rule her.

Orla clutched the sides of Ann's head, muttering strange words of power.

Ann squeezed her eyes shut. Her mental shield would hold. Darius had spent weeks of teaching her to protect her mind.

"They may break your body, but you must never let them touch your mind," he said.

She felt Orla trying to claw her way into her head and chip away at the wall around her thoughts. Her father's training had never failed her before, and she wouldn't let it now.

Ann imagined herself in the training courtyard where she used to practice with Ed every day, indulging her dream of being one of the Black. Ed had even bought her the very black cloak they had taken from her because it was similar to what the other Black wore. He'd used it to cover her when her family had been massacred. Now she wore it as a reminder of that.

Orla went at it for hours, but Ann's shield held.

Ann slumped back in the metal chair, laughing through the blood that poured from her nose. "Is that the best you can do?" she asked. "You won't break me. You might have destroyed Rhiannon, but I'm not her anymore."

"Fine, if pain won't work on you, let's see how you feel about me hurting someone else." Orla snapped her fingers, and Ceara dragged Xander into the room.

Ann's heart skipped at the sight of her brother. He looked haggard. One eye was swollen shut, his nose sat at an odd angle, and burns covered every inch of visible skin.

"Ann?" He looked up and shook his head. "No, I told you…"

"Enough!" Orla snapped. "Ceara, start putting some holes in him."

Ceara drew one of her knives and jabbed it through Xander's throat.

"Tell me where Urien is, or I will make you watch your brother die a thousand times," Orla hissed.

"I can't tell you what I don't know," Ann snapped.

"Fine. Ceara, hold him." Orla grabbed an empty bottle, smashed it, and pierced the side of his leg. "A little deeper and he'll bleed out."

Xander gurgled through a mouthful of blood as Ceara held him upright.

Ann tried to look away, but another Gliss turned her head and forced her to watch.

"I'll torture him until you give me what I want," Orla growled.

Xander's head slumped forward, and his breathing stilled.

"I told you, I don't know."

"Fine." Orla grabbed another bottle, handing it to one of the other Gliss, who poured its contents over Xander's body. The smell of alcohol filled the air.

"Let's see how well Darius' spell works now," Orla said as fire sparked between her fingers.

CHAPTER 17

Ann felt tears prick her eyes as a red-hot inferno enveloped Xander's body, the flames licking their way through flesh and bone. They made their way from his shoulders, down his arms, to his torso and then his legs, consuming everything in their wake. His cries of agony filled the air, tearing into Ann's heart. His skin turned black, flesh smouldering as his body slumped to the floor.

Ann closed her eyes, unable to bear any more. Fire was her element. If they had set her ablaze, she would probably have stayed unharmed. Why couldn't Orla have attacked her? They'd both died several times over the years, but never like this. Usually, death came at the end of a blade.

Hours seemed to pass as the smell of burning flesh filled the room, reminding her of a pig roasting over a fire.

Ann had cried so much those first few months after losing her parents, she thought she'd never have any more tears left to shed. The door banged shut, and she opened her eyes to find the charred body of her brother, and she let out a strangled sob. She tugged at her restraints, not caring when they dug into her wrists and ankles like barbed wire and pulling hard until they finally broke. She yanked one wrist free, then the other, before pulling away the bonds around her ankles. Her hands were bruised and bloodied. She rubbed them on her trousers and crawled over to her brother, the cold hard stone bruising her already torn flesh.

"Xander? Xander, wake up, please." The tears flowed freely now.

His face looked almost unrecognisable beneath red welts and blackened flesh. The spell she'd always hated her father for casting now had to work. It had to bring her brother back.

"Come on, little brother, wake up." Ann clutched his blackened hand. His fingers felt hard and stiff in hers. "You can't die, not like this. Xander!"

She closed her eyes and clung to him. He'd always been there for her, even after Darius had been cruel to him. She couldn't lose him.

The door creaked open, and Ann glared up at Ceara. "Come to gloat, have you?" If she were stronger, she would've killed the Gliss with her bare hands.

Ceara flinched. "No, I came to check on the—"

"On the body? If he doesn't come back from this, you'll have no leverage!" she cried. "Why couldn't you have just tortured me instead? I'm the one who killed Urien." She wiped tears away with the back of her hand.

"This wouldn't have had to happen if you told us where Urien is." Ceara avoided meeting her gaze. She wouldn't look at Xander either.

"I already told you, *I don't know*. I made sure no one would ever find him!" Ann screamed. "Get out, I don't want to look at you anymore. You helped murder my family."

"I didn't kill Darius or Deanna; I was just an onlooker." Ceara hesitated as she walked to the door. "For what it's worth, I'm sorry."

"Sorry?" Ann snorted. "You're a Gliss. You don't know the meaning of sorry."

"Xander was kind to me. I loved him once," Ceara said. "Try to understand, I just want my love back."

"Urien doesn't love you. He doesn't know how to love anyone but himself. Get away from me."

To her surprise, Ceara left without saying another word. Ann wanted to rip her apart. She might not have set Xander aflame, but she was just as guilty as Orla.

I should've known the night she came to us was a trick. Sage should've warned us instead of believing Ceara's lies. Even Ed had wanted to believe she'd changed, but she never would. She'd proved that by siding with Urien in the first place.

Ann wiped her eyes. All plans of her escape faded. Nothing mattered without Xander. Nothing. She'd kill Orla for this somehow. She'd have revenge.

Ann clutched her head once again as light and sound exploded inside her brain just as they had when Ceara touched her earlier.

Ann, I'm sorry for the pain, but this is the only way I can talk to you without Orla or anyone else finding out. Ceara's voice rang through her ears. *I know you think I'm a traitor, but it's time you finally saw the truth.*

She winced as images flashed by of Ceara sneaking out to see them. Of her talking to Sage many times over the years, warning her of Orla's plans, of her torturing Xander, then Edward.

All the images were followed by feelings of pain, sadness, and regret at her betrayal. Ceara missed her family. Ann's temples throbbed as the series of images finally ended and the cell door banged shut behind Ceara.

Xander gasped as his eyes opened.

"Oh, thank the spirits!" Ann breathed, hugging him tight.

"Ann…what…?" Xander asked, struggling for breath.

"It's okay, I'm here. I've never been so glad for Papa's spell." She watched as the burns began to fade, replaced by pale flesh. "I've got to get you out of here."

"Sage—"

"Shush. You need to rest. They'll be back once they realise they can still use you against me."

"Ann…Gliss…Trin." He struggled to get the words out.

"Trin? But the Gliss can't find Trin. The island is always moving."

"Found it. Not…Safe."

Ann sat up, more determined than ever to escape now she knew she had to protect her people. "I've got to think. We used to play here as children, do you remember another way out of the dungeons?"

Xander ran his finger over the floor, tracing a word in the dirt: *'Death'*.

"Yes, I'd rather not think of that right now. For a few awful moments, I thought I'd lost you forever."

"Out." He pointed at the word. "Way…out."

Ann frowned and wiped the word away. "Are you saying death is a way out?" she whispered in his ear.

Xander nodded and gripped her hand. "Get…Message…Out."

"That *was* you I saw earlier. You were trying to warn me!" She picked up a shard of the smashed bottle off the floor. "See you soon," she said, slicing her throat.

Ann blinked as she appeared in the dark gloom of the other side. *Okay, here I am.*

She hated coming to this place every time she died.

"Ann?" Xander appeared beside her.

"Xander, you shouldn't be here. You're weak enough already." Despite her admonishment, she wrapped her arms around him.

"I need to talk to you without fear of anyone overhearing us. As I was trying to tell you back there, Orla sent the Gliss to Trin. They might already be there." Xander returned her embrace, then pulled away. "You need to focus and project yourself to Sage."

Ann closed her eyes and thought of Sage but didn't move. "Nothing's happening. Maybe it's because my body is still bound."

"Those bracelets affect the body, not the spirit. Come on, Ann. You can do this." He took her hand. "*We* can do this."

"I can't keep watching them kill you. I told Orla the truth, I don't remember what I did with Urien's body. I banished his soul, but I don't know where. I erased the memory from my mind."

"What about his body?"

She shook her head. "Edward dealt with that, but I erased those memories too."

"Then just concentrate on warning Sage now. Hurry!"

Ann closed her eyes, drew magic, and thought of Trin.

Light blinded her as she reappeared in the altar room inside the tower. The walls around her trembled, and shouts rang out.

"Sage?" she called. "Sage!"

Sage hurried into the room. "Rhiannon, what are you doing here?" she asked. "We're under attack."

"I projected. Listen, you, Flo, and anyone else here on the island needs to leave." Ann glanced around, half expecting the Gliss to come bursting in.

"Orla has you, doesn't she?" Sage gasped. "How did that happen?"

"Yes, but don't worry about that, just get to safety. I can't let her use anyone else I care about as leverage," Ann said. "Orla won't stop until she finds Urien."

"We'll get out, but you must get away from her. I'll—"

"No, don't worry about me. Just go."

Sage moved to the door. "Remember, you are much more powerful than her, and Orla knows that. Use that power."

Ann blinked, surprised to find herself back in the darkness of limbo. The chill of the mist crept into her very soul as she scanned it for Xander, who had vanished. She guessed he'd returned to his body, and waited, expecting to feel the call of her own, but nothing happened. Ann frowned. She'd never stayed dead for this long.

Something must be preventing me from going back, she realised. *Damn it, I need to go back to my body, but maybe I can get a message to someone else.*

Edward, she thought.

Ann gasped as she reappeared in another room that looked almost as dark as the other side. "Ed?"

Ed spun around and gasped. "Ann, how—?"

"No time to explain. You need to go to Trin and save Flo and Sage. The Gliss are— where are you?" She glanced around.

"In the crypt below the city where I buried Urien's body."

"I erased those memories from your mind!"

"The spell didn't work, but you know I'd never betray you, which is why I'm doing what I should have done all those years ago."

"Wait, what *are* you doing?" she asked as he pulled a bottle from the rucksack he wore and poured its contents over the sarcophagus.

Ann leaned closer, spotting the face of her elder brother Urien. He looked almost peaceful.

"Ed, no! He can't die either, remember?"

"If there's no body he can never come back. Now, Jax!"

On cue, Jax said words of power and threw a fireball.

Ann screamed as pain ripped through her chest and her spirit form started to waver.

"No!" Ed made a grab for her hand. "You need to tell me where you are."

"Palace…" she gasped, and everything went black.

When Ann awoke, she found herself lying within a circle. Runes had been drawn on the floor, and their power held her in place. She tried to sit up, only to have an invisible force push her back down.

"Now, let's get to retrieving those memories, shall we?" Orla asked.

CHAPTER 18

Edward glanced around, half hoping to see the projection of Ann still there but found no sign of her. His heart twisted with disappointment. He'd been desperate to find her ever since she disappeared, and worry for her had made controlling the beast a constant battle. He should have known that Ursaie woman had been someone in disguise out to prey on Ann's sense of justice, but he had been too far away for his beast side to smell or sense any sign of deceit.

In the end, logic had won over his heart. Instead of trying to find her, he had decided to go straight to Urien's body. The deceptive plot to capture Ann had Orla written all over it. It had taken a while to dig up his buried memories of that day. But, deep down, he'd always known where he'd hidden the body. Ann wouldn't have of wanted him wasting time trying to find her. She'd want him to do the right thing.

He felt sure Ann would do everything she could to fight off Orla's attempts at reading her mind to search for Urien's location. But if Orla did somehow figure out what had happened to Urien, it would only be only a matter of time before she came in search of his body. So Edward would make sure there was no body left to find.

He glanced down at the tomb of hard rock that had encased Urien's body for all these years after they had escaped from the palace. He frowned, disappointed that it had resisted their attempt at cremation. In hindsight, the night he brought Urien here had been the first time he'd noticed his beast strength. Ed had always known he was different but had never given it much thought. He and Flora's other fosterlings knew very little about where they had originally come from. They were considered the rogues of magic. Most of them were the unwanted product of the forbidden intermingling of different races. Finding their families had never been important to any of them. Even if they tried, most of them would either be killed or turned away.

Ed reluctantly shoved the last stone back in place. It glittered with the same runes he'd cast all those years ago to seal Urien's body inside and stop anyone from being able to trace it, which he'd learnt from Ann.

"Ann didn't seem too happy about you trying to destroy Urien's body," Jax remarked. "It makes sense, though. How can his body be destroyed when he is protected by Darius' spell?"

"I hope she's okay," he replied.

"I get the feeling she can take care of herself," Jax said. "We need to get to Trin and hurry. Sage and Flo won't stand much of a chance against the Gliss."

Ed started drew symbols within a circle—the signs of transference. "You'll have to say the words," Ed told him. "I've only got limited power thanks to the beast."

Jax hesitated. "But I'm a shifter. The changing state of my energy means I can't cast complex spells, let alone use transference magic. Ann always used to transport us when we needed to go somewhere."

"You can do it. All Black had to be able to transfer themselves from one place to another, remember?" He stepped inside the circle. "Just focus on where you want to go."

Jax stepped inside after him, still hesitant. "It's been a long time since I went to Trin."

"It doesn't matter, you need to concentrate." He tried not to show his impatience. The only thing he could think of was getting to Ann, but she'd asked him to help Sage and Flo, and he'd do just that. "Picture the shore along the river. The reeds..."

Jax raised his hand and said words of power. Familiar light flashed, and Ed and Jax went tumbling to the ground, Ed almost falling into the river as they landed. He caught his footing easily, noticing his reflexes were much faster than they used to be—another sign of the beast, no doubt.

"Told you I wasn't very good." Jax waded out of the water where he'd fallen, muttering a curse under his breath.

"It's okay, we're here." He raised his hand, said the incantation, and waited for the reeds to start moving, but nothing happened.

Had he lost all his power now? He frowned, glancing at his hands. The beast grumbled in the back of his mind, but it hadn't stopped him from summoning the boat when he and Ann had visited the island a few days earlier.

"Jax, you try."

Jax gestured and chanted the words to summon the boat.

Again, nothing. The reeds didn't so much as stir. Ed couldn't understand it. He'd never known this to happen before. If Ann were here, she might have known what was wrong.

"Maybe Sage sealed off the island to stop the Gliss from getting there?"

Ed shook his head. "No, it wouldn't do much good. Something's not right."

"We could transport ourselves there, couldn't we?" Jax gave him a pointed look. "Didn't Darius transport himself to the island? Did Ann ever show you how to do that?"

"Only the archdruid can do that. The wards keep everyone else out."

"Isn't there another way in?"

Ed rubbed his chin, trying to remember. "The island is sacred for the druids, which we aren't."

"We were raised by a druid and among druids. They must have another way on and off the island." Jax glanced over at the heavy veil of mist in the distance. "Think! Ann must have told you something. She used to tell you everything about her magic, and she is one of the few Magickind who could transport herself to different locations."

Ed thought back. "I think there was an old tunnel. Flo used to tell stories about how the druids escaped when the island got invaded after one of the realm wars. It's a passage that led under the island, but I don't know where it is."

"Good, use your beast and find it."

Ed frowned. "How do you know so much about this beast?"

"I saw a lot when Orla held me captive, and I learnt a lot too. You're stronger and faster than any man. You should be able to see clearer," Jax said. "Stop resisting it and use it."

He sighed. "I don't sense anything."

"Why not let the beast take control again?"

He shook his head. "I can't. What if it fully takes control and I can't come back?" He didn't want to risk losing control. Especially not when he knew Ann was in danger. No doubt the beast would take off and try to find her.

"The beast is part of you."

"Fine. Be careful, I don't want you or anyone else to get hurt."

Ed closed his eyes and dropped his mental wall. The moment he did, his eyes burned. His fangs elongated, and his claws came out. He felt the beast's exhilaration at freedom and the need to hunt.

An image of Ann flashed through his mind, and the beast glanced around, searching for her.

Not Ann, find Sage and Flo, he thought. *Find a way to Trin. Look for a tunnel.*

The beast growled, then took off along the embankment. Colours and sounds whirled past as Ed ran faster than he ever had before. It felt strangely exhilarating to move at such a high speed, but no longer dizzying or disorientating as it had when he'd first started

"Hey, wait for me!" Jax yelled. "I can't move as fast as you can!"

Ed tried to stop but couldn't. He hated not being in control of his own body, a presence in a creature he couldn't communicate with.

The beast didn't have thoughts, only primal feelings. Right now, it was overtaken with the need to hunt, to kill.

He looked to the ground, which had shimmered in various greens and browns around purple lines of magical energy deep within the earth. Erthea lines.

Jax appeared beside him in his crow form. *You move bloody fast*, he breathed. *Ed, are you still there?*

"Yes," his voice came out low and guttural.

Good. See, I said you could control it. Annoying you can move faster than I can fly, though.

Ed ignored him, spotting a large void in the pattern on the ground. When he stamped on it, it sounded hollow. Willing the beast to move, he bent and pulled a hidden door off its hinges. He tossed it aside and jumped into the darkness below.

Ed landed easily, breathing in the salty air from the sea above.

Jax flew down beside him and shifted back into human form. "Good job, mate. I knew you could do it."

Ed grunted and took off down the tunnel.

"Hey, what about waiting for me?" Jax called.

He ignored him and moved away in a blur. He could sense danger in the air. Blood pumped through him, and the faster he moved, the stronger the feeling became.

"Ed!" Jax yelled. "I could get bloody lost down here!"

Ed sniffed. Among the salt and seaweed, he caught the coppery scent of blood.

Sage! Ed thought and said, *Hurry, Jax, we can't let anything happen to her.*

"I'm getting too old for this," Jax puffed. "Do you have to keep running off without me?"

Don't be stupid, you're only twenty-seven. I can't control how fast I move. It just happens.

Ed took off again, running faster until he reached the end of the tunnel. He leapt, bursting through the hatch to land on solid ground. Up ahead, he spotted Flo being dragged through a portal that was held open by a guard.

Ed moved so fast he blurred, heading straight for the first Gliss he spotted. This one was blonde and dark-eyed. She blocked his first blow then kicked out at him.

He grunted, but the blow didn't hurt as much as he'd expected it to. He countered her next move easily, knocking a knife from her hand. His only thought was of finding and reaching Sage and Flo.

Jax appeared through the hatch in human form and drew his staff, hitting the first Gliss that came at him.

Ed knocked his Gliss to the ground but could only watch as the remaining Gliss and the guard vanished through the portal with Flo.

We're too late. Damn it! That was our last chance to save them. Rage heated his blood, and Ed felt what little he had control he had over the beast start to slip away.

"Whoa, your eyes are turning red. Ed, you need to stay focused," Jax told him.

He growled. He didn't want to focus, he wanted blood, revenge on the people who'd taken his foster mother away.

"Edward?" called another voice.

He turned to see Sage running toward them.

"Phew, you're okay," Jax breathed.

"They took Flora," Sage said, her breaths coming sharp and short. "They came looking for the key."

"The key to what?" Jax frowned and glanced at Ed. "I think he's losing control again, Sage." "The key to a box which holds the crystal containing Urien's soul. Ann gave it to me the night of the revolution. It's my own fault, I should never have transported it back here. I hoped you'd get here in time to—never mind. We're too late."

Ed's fists clenched tight, his claws digging into his palms as he fought for control. *It's my body, I'm in control.*

He felt the beast's resistance, its reluctance to go back into the cage of his mind. It wanted to stay out, to control his body. Above all, it wanted Ann, but its emotions toward her confused him. It shared his desire to protect her, that much he could tell.

He winced as the fangs and claws finally retreated. It hurt every time.

"What about Urien's body?" he asked. "We couldn't destroy that, and if they get to it…"

"I cast a spell that removed his heart to stop anyone bringing him back even if his body and soul were recovered. But it's only a matter of time before they find that." Sage shook her head. "I failed. I should never have let Rhiannon go after Xander."

"You didn't *let* Ann do anything. We all knew this would happen one day." Ed ran a hand through his hair. "We've just been delaying the inevitable."

"What's our next move? Go to the city and try to free Ann?" Jax asked.

"No, I'm the only one who knows where Urien's body lies. We have to go there." He visualised the graveyard he and Jax had visited earlier. "Sage, will you cast a transference spell?"

After Sage invoked the circle, the three of them reappeared on the outskirts of the graveyard, in a section he'd never seen before. The ancient tombs had been built raised off the ground. They loomed like dark sentinels, silent and foreboding.

"How do you remember where you hid Urien's body?" Sage asked. "Rhiannon erased your memory."

Ed hesitated. "It didn't work, but I buried that memory deep so only I could reach it."

"What if Orla—?"

"Orla didn't touch it. She broke my body, but she didn't reach that far into my mind."

"You don't remember what Orla did to you," Jax pointed out.

"But I would know if she'd found the body—we all would." Ed stalked through the graveyard. The air smelt of wet grass and dark leaves covered the ground. Beneath the earth and soil, he could detect the scent of decay but ignored it.

"Do you think it's possible to destroy Urien's body after all?" asked Jax, catching up with him. "What if it affects Ann and Xander?"

"No, but if I can't destroy it, then I have to make sure it goes somewhere Orla can never find it."

CHAPTER 19

Ann screamed as pain tore through her mind. Orla had been at it for hours, but Ann wouldn't lower her mental shield. Blood dripped from her nose, sliding down her face. "Haven't you figured out this isn't going to work yet?" She glared at Orla.

"I will find my son," Orla hissed. "And discover whatever you did to him." She turned and swept out of the room, the door banging behind her.

Moments later, Xander groaned from where he lay slumped in the corner.

"Are you alright?" Ann asked, blinking as her vision began to return—the pain had blinded her.

Xander nodded. "I'm healing, but I ache everywhere." He blinked, raising his head. "Why do you think Papa bound us so we don't die?"

Ann shifted in the uncomfortable chair they had shackled her to. "I think he suspected Urien might turn against him, and this was his way of making sure Urien didn't kill us."

"How many times do you think we can cheat death before it becomes permanent?"

Ann shook her head. "I don't know, little brother. I didn't know Papa even knew how to use such powerful magic. Defying death goes against nature itself."

"I don't want to live forever, Ann, especially when I'm not *living*. I'm hiding. I often wonder what our lives would have been like if it weren't for what happened, if we didn't have to run," Xander said. "I'm tired of running."

"I know, I am too. Little good it's done us. What do you think you would have become if things hadn't happened?"

"I don't know, perhaps a bard, or a scholar. I never wanted to be a warrior, that's not who I am."

"I wanted to join the Black—not to protect Papa, but because I loved how they stood for freedom, honour, and unity." Ann rested her head against the cold hard metal of her chair. "Papa wanted me to be his heir. I heard him and Urien arguing about it that night. Sometimes I feel like what happened is my fault."

"Don't be daft. Urien is the one who did this, not you. *He's* the reason we ended up here."

"What happened to him? He was our brother. He played with us, brought us gifts…." She'd often wondered where it all gone wrong, and when he'd stopped being their brother.

"I think power went to his head. Just like it did with Papa. But Papa could handle it and Urien couldn't," Xander said. "I don't even remember what happened that night. I know I walked in on them arguing, but I passed out after Orla stabbed me."

Ann tugged at her restraints. *If I could die again, maybe I could call Ed and find out if Sage and Flo are safe.*

"What do *you* remember?" Xander asked. "What did you do to stop Urien?" He rested back against the wall to hold his body upright. "I still wonder about him. He's still our brother."

"I erased those memories from my mind. Anyway, I try not to think about him. We've moved on."

"Yeah, but for a while, after it happened, I worried I'd lose you."

Ann flinched. It had been a dark time when they'd first gone into hiding. She struggled with what happened and had shut down her emotions. In the end, she learnt to live with the pain, though she would never get over it.

"There must be another way out. If I could just get loose…"

"I doubt I'd get far. My body is still weak." Xander rested his head against the wall. "They'll keep torturing us."

"We'll find a way out. Ed will come."

"You love him, don't you?"

"Of course I do, he's my best friend."

"No. I meant you're *in* love with him, aren't you?"

Ann didn't answer and instead tried to think of the best escape route. "When a Gliss comes in, do you think you could grab one of her knives? Your hands are free to move, and mine aren't."

"They'd stop me before I had the chance to grab anything. Where was Ceara after Papa and Urien fought?" Xander asked. "I keep trying to remember what happened. How did we get out of the palace?"

"Why would you want to remember any of it?" She frowned at him. They still spoke of their parents often, but never that night. It was best forgotten.

"Because it might help us get out of here."

Sighing, Ann closed her eyes and let memory drag her in.

Ann woke to the sound of shouting. Rubbing her eyes, she got out of bed, brushing her hair off her face as she padded across the room. It had to be after midnight. Papa must be working late, but who would he be arguing with?

The sound of something breaking made her jump as she reached for the handle of her bedroom door. She tugged at it, yet it wouldn't open. She frowned. The door could only be locked from the inside, and no one could get into her room to do so. Her wards wouldn't allow it.

Ann raised her hand and motioned for the door to open. Again, nothing happened. Her magic rippled uselessly against the door. Her eyes narrowed. Why was she trapped inside?

She tugged at the handle again, this time using both her physical strength and magical power to force it open. Again, it refused to budge.

She stepped back and raised her hands, blasting the door with her power. Fire exploded against the wood. The door flashed with light and remained intact. *What is going on?*

Ann raised her hands again, blasting the door over and over until it creaked open.

She hurried down the hallway that led to her father's meeting chamber. Raised voices echoed through the air, along with the sounds of a struggle. Her parents rarely argued, and it wouldn't have turned violent even if they were.

Fear forming a knot in her stomach, she moved down the hall, surprised to find no guards around.

Someone screamed. Ann froze, unsure what to do next.

"No!" cried another voice that she recognised as her father's.

By the spirits, what's happening? She ran down the corridor and steps to the floor below, toward the sound of the voice. On the floor by the doors to her father's chamber lay her mother, a knife protruding from her chest.

"Mama?" Ann gasped, falling to her knees beside her. She touched her mother's neck but found no pulse.

Xander rushed into the hall, freezing at the scene. "Mama? Mama, no!" He fell to his knees. "What happened? Who did this?"

Ann shook her head. "I don't know. I couldn't get to her in time." Tears rolled down her cheeks. "I've got to find Papa."

"No!" Xander wailed. "She can't die."

"Xander, listen to me. We can't help Mama now, she's gone. I'll find Papa." She gripped his shoulders. "You need to go and find Edward. Don't trust anyone else. Get somewhere safe."

"We can't just leave her here!"

"We won't. I'll come back for her, I promise." Ann hugged him. "Papa will know what to do, he'll find a way to bring her back."

Ann ran towards her father's chamber, tears streaming down her face. She opened the door to see Urien and Darius fighting and ran

241

into the room. Before she could defend her father, the sound of Xander screaming filtered down the hallway. She turned and rushed back toward the doors. A shadowy figure lunged at her. *Orla.*

Ann raised her hand, hitting her father's former mistress in the chest with a fireball.

Orla stumbled backward and bared her teeth. "My son will not be denied his birthright!"

More fire flared in Ann's hand, and she hurled it at the other woman, sending her crashing across the room, where she lay unmoving

Ann turned to see Darius and Urien continue to struggle over a knife. She threw a ball of fire at her brother just as her father crumpled to his knees, burned and bleeding. From the doorway, a knife flew towards Urien. Ann turned to see Xander lying on the floor, blood pouring from a wound in his stomach.

"Ann?" His eyes closed. He went limp as Ceara, kneeling behind him, let out a quiet sob.

"Xander!" Ann knelt beside him.

Blood gurgled from his throat, his life draining away.

This couldn't be happening. All around her, her family lay either dead or dying. Tears swam across her vision as she looked at Ceara. "*You.*"

Ceara shook her head. "I didn't—Orla…"

With a scream of anguish, Ann used her fire to blast Ceara from the room. Letting go of Xander, she rounded on Urien. "Why would you do this?" she screamed. "Why?"

Urien's eyes burned red. "He said I wasn't his heir. That I'm a bastard and have no legitimate claim to the role of archdruid," he said. "He said *you* were his heir."

"It's just a bloody title, it doesn't mean anything!" Ann cried. "You didn't need to kill them! They are our parents, Urien!"

"*Your* parents, not mine. I've been waiting years for him to name me his heir!"

"Rhiannon…"

She scrambled over to their bleeding father. "Papa, you're going to be fine. I'll heal you."

She drew magic, but Darius shoved her hand away. "Rhiannon, go. Get out of here!"

"No, I can save you!"

"You must be strong. Remember everything I've taught you...Live for me." His chest heaved as he struggled to draw in a breath.

She closed her eyes, letting the tears fall.

"Rhiannon, you don't have to meet the same fate as them," Urien said. "You're the only one who doesn't deserve to die. You've always been kind to me."

"When were Xander or my mother ever unkind to you?" Ann snarled. "She took you in and treated you like family, and this is how you repay her."

"I was the bastard of the family to everyone but you," Urien said. "Join me, and together we'll create a new order and rule the five lands."

Ann ripped off a piece of her nightgown, pressing it against her father's wounds. *Hold on, Papa. I'm going to save you.*

Don't waste your power on me. You have to stop Urien and Orla with everything you have left. Darius told her. *You must let me go.*

I can't. I won't, she replied, rising to her feet. *Just hold on.*

"All you've ever wanted is power." Ann circled her brother as fire flared in her hand.

Orla rose from where she had fallen to leap at her, and Ann hurled it, sending the murdering bitch hurtling through the window.

"Rhiannon, together we could have more power than you could ever imagine," Urien's eyes gleamed. He remained where he stood, unconcerned about his mother. "Think about it. We'd be unstoppable."

"I have power. I want my family back." This time, she threw a fireball at him.

Urien dodged it, his hands still wet with her parents' blood. "So be it." Lightning formed in his own hand.

They both had strong elemental magic. Ann's powers came from nature, Urien's seemed to come from the very depths of the underworld.

This time she raised both her hands, bright red sparks flaring as fire surged across the room.

Urien winced as he struggled to deflect her magic. As Ann poured her pain, her anger, her grief into her power, her fire burned hotter than it had before. Another tide made Urien stagger backwards until he was against a wall. "You won't kill me, you're not a killer."

Ann readied herself for another blast. She didn't care. She wanted him to suffer, to burn, to pay for killing the people she loved the most.

"No!" Darius struggled to his feet, blood seeping through his shirt. "I won't let you kill each other."

"Papa?" Ann turned, and Urien took the opportunity to blast her across the room.

Darius' lips moved as he chanted silent words of power, then Ann screamed as white-hot lightning shot across the room, striking her, Urien, and Xander in the chest.

Pain radiated through her entire body, and she was left feeling like her soul had been torn apart.

She heard Urien screaming and knew he experienced the same agony. That gave her some small comfort.

Silence and eerie stillness followed.

Ann took a deep breath, then another, surprised to find herself still alive. She crawled over to her father, tears streaming down her face. "Papa, please wake up. You can't leave," she said. "I need you!"

Darius reached up to touch her cheek. "You'll be safe," he whispered. "You three will forever be bound by blood." He smiled, then his hand fell away as life left him.

She let out an anguished sob. "No, come back!"

Urien sprang back up. "What did he do to me?"

Ann let go of her father's hand, stared up at her brother, and rose. "You did this. You killed them." She raised her hand, letting her power free.

Urien gasped as smoke wrapped around his throat. "You can't kill me, I am—"

"Oh, I'll do worse than that, brother. Death is too kind for you, and as you said, I'm not a killer," she replied. "Instead, I banish you."

Urien struggled, gasping for breath as he tried to fight back. "I'm...the archdruid."

"If you were, you would have stopped me already," Ann said.

Urien sank to his knees, still in the grip of her power. "You can't do this," he hissed. "I'm your brother."

"Yes, and you killed my little brother and my parents. They were my family, and you took them from me. Now I'll make sure you never harm anyone again." She flung out her hand, and Urien screamed as she yanked his spirit from his body.

Ann chanted words of power, reaching out beyond time and space to cast his soul into the abyss. She drew runes in the air, sealing the spell. Urien's body vanished as she sent it away too.

Ann sank to her knees as all power and energy faded from her.

"What have you done?" Orla cried as she appeared in the doorway. "Where's my son?"

Ann smiled despite the emptiness she felt. "Somewhere you'll never find him."

The sound of laughter made the memory fade. Ann blinked and saw Orla standing over her.

"Thank you." Orla grinned. "You've just given me exactly what I needed."

CHAPTER 20

"No!" Ann screamed as the Gliss reached into the shadows and dragged an unconscious Xander from the room, slamming the cell door shut. She couldn't believe it. Orla had tricked her by using her demon powers to pose as her brother and reliving that horrific night had brought all her memories back. *How could I be so stupid? I should have known it wasn't Xander.*

Blaming herself was useless. Orla now knew how to bring Urien back.

At least they would still need his body and heart. Only Ed knew where the body lay, and Sage had hidden the heart.

Ann had to get another message to Ed, but that would mean dying again.

She worked on freeing her hand when the door swung open, and Ceara came in.

"Where's my brother?" Ann demanded.

"He's being tended to. I've come to move you; it's almost time for the ritual."

Her eyes narrowed. "What ritual?"

"The ritual needed for Urien come back." Ceara smiled.

"She can't—"

"Orla has everything she needs. Urien and I will finally be together again." Ceara undid the restraints, and Ann lunged.

Ceara blocked the blow, grabbed Ann's wrist and yanked one arm back, then the other. "Fighting is pointless, Ann. Urien will return. There's nothing you can do to stop it."

"You can't do this. You know as well as anyone Urien can't come back."

She's probably the one who used her power to get me to relive Urien's final moments. She stabbed us in the back again.

Ceara dragged Ann down the hall, pulling her into a large room. Torches were lit around them, and two circles had been carved into the floor. Xander was positioned on a table in the centre of one, still unconscious.

"Urien won't care if you've been loyal to him or not," she told Ceara.

Ceara scoffed. "Of course he will. I've talked to him when I've connected to the spirit world. He loves me, and he misses me as much as I miss him."

Ann tried not to roll her eyes. "I know what he's like with women. He'll never love you. Plus, I saw how you were with Xander."

Ceara's dark eyes flashed. "What did you see?"

"You care about him more than you should," Ann said. "Gliss don't show compassion, they're trained not to feel any emotion except hate or anger."

"You know nothing." Ceara struck her across the face, making Ann's head reel back.

Ann winced but didn't cry out. Ceara shoved her inside the circle, and light flashed. She tried to move, only to have a burst of lightning knock her to the ground.

Orla came in, surrounded by several other Gliss. "It's time my son came back and took his rightful place as ruler of all the lands." She approached the circle and shoved a metal spike through Ann's shoulder.

Ann doubled over as pain tore through her and dozens of cuts appeared over her arms and legs. Orla's power burned her skin, cutting and slashing as it went. Blood dripped down and flowed through the circle as Orla began to chant.

Ann tried to move and slumped backwards, powerless to do anything. Every time she tried, an invisible force pushed her back down.

More and more blood flowed, running along the floor and into the circle where Xander lay.

"Xander, wake up!" she cried.

"He can't hear you," Orla called as she pulled something from a small wooden box.

Ann's limbs refused to move no matter how much she tried, weighing her down.

"Xander, please wake up," she begged, noticing for the first time that his skin was intact. Why weren't they draining his blood too?

She gasped as realisation dawned. They were going to put Urien's heart inside Xander's body and use him as a vessel to house Urien's soul.

"You can't do this to him!" Ann screamed. "I'll kill you for this."

"Urien needs a body, someone with Valeran blood. Xander's the perfect candidate," said Orla. "You only have yourself to blame. If I had Urien's body, I wouldn't need your brother."

"I'll tell you where it is. Just don't do this to him!"

Orla snorted. "I know you don't know the whereabouts of Urien's resting place, and I need my son by my side. With the unrest growing by the day, the people need Urien to unite the lands."

"Do you really think Urien will keep you around?" Ann hissed. "He's only ever wanted power; he won't let anything get in the way of getting it. Not even you will be safe from him."

Orla laughed. "He's my son. I taught him everything, including how to kill," she said. "Enjoy your last moments while you can, the first thing I'll have him do is kill you. Your blood will break the bond that Darius made all those years ago."

Orla moved away and reached into Xander's chest, which had been sliced open.

"Xander, please wake up!" Ann begged, tugging at her restraints.

Xander's eyes flew open as Orla yanked his heart out and placed Urien's inside his chest. Light flashed over him as she did so, knitting the flesh over his torso back together.

"No!" Exhausted, Ann's scream came out as a whisper.

Blue light filled the air, long tendrils of mist swirling in every direction as it shot into Xander's body.

Ann closed her eyes and turned away. She didn't need her powers to know that was Urien's soul.

Orla reached into the circle, grabbing hold of her and forcing her to look as Xander rose, an eerie fire in his eyes.

But it wasn't Xander anymore. It was Urien. It sickened her to see him looking back at her through Xander's eyes. She had no idea what he would do to her now. Would he want revenge?

Ann didn't care what he or they did to her. She had to find a way to save Xander. To do that, she needed to escape. To restore her strength and her magic.

"Hello, sister," Urien's voice came out low and harsh. Xander's eyes flashed with power.

Orla wrapped her arms around him. "Welcome home, my boy. It's good to have you back. I promised you I'd never give up on you." She cupped his face. "You can finally take your place as leader of the lands."

Urien wrapped an arm around her and held her for a moment. "Thank you, Mother. Without you, I'd never have gotten free of that hell." He pulled away. "I knew you'd help me find a way back."

"We have much to do." Orla said, "but first, I thought you'd want to take care of this problem." She motioned to Ann, handing Urien a knife.

Tears streamed down Ann's cheeks, her only concern for her little brother. She had no idea if Xander had been banished, killed, or if he was still trapped inside his body somewhere. "Just do it," she said.

Urien knelt and whispered, "I'll see you again soon, sister."

Then he plunged the knife through her chest.

The cold hard metal ripped through flesh, glancing off her ribs as he pushed the blade deep until it finally found her heart. Then blackness consumed her.

Ann felt herself floating as she reappeared in the gloom of limbo. Great, she'd expected herself to move on to wherever spirits went after they experienced true death, yet here she was again. The mists flowed around her, feeling like eyes staring. Waiting to see what happened next.

Now what? she wondered. Would she linger here until she faded into oblivion? She didn't think she had any unfinished business, so why hadn't she moved on?

Xander? If his spirit had been forced out, he should be here too. "Xander, are you here?"

Ann moved around, seeing nothing but darkness. Was her concern for Xander holding her here? *Xander is gone. I'm ready to go. I should have died five years ago, but now is my time to move on.*

She waited, but nothing happened.

*Why isn't it working? I'm ready to be with my family again. Unless I'm not dead…*Ann closed her eyes and felt the pull of her body but couldn't return. *The knife must still be in me. Wonderful. Let's hope they remove it, or I'm stuck here.*

What about Ed? Maybe he and Jax could help.

Ann closed her eyes and willed herself somewhere else.

Ann gasped as she took a deep breath, her lungs burning for air as she opened her eyes. Ceara and Urien were still in the room with her, so she made her body go still.

"I'm so happy to have you back." Ceara kissed Urien, smiling. "I missed you so much."

Urien caressed Ceara's cheek and pulled away. "Doesn't it bother you that I no longer have my true face?"

"It doesn't matter what face you have as long as we're together." Ceara wrapped her arms, but Urien brushed her off.

"I watched you when I was trapped on the other side. You cared for my brother, didn't you?" he snarled.

"Of course not. I—"

"Liar!" Urien struck Ceara so hard blood dripped from her nose.

Now that's the Urien I know—the one who killed my parents. Don't say I didn't warn you, Ceara. Ann looked away. It made her sick to see Urien's soul looking out through the eyes of Xander.

"He…he was kind to me," Ceara said, wiping her face with the back of her hand.

"Gliss are taught to forego such emotions. You've gone soft in my absence, and I can't have any weaknesses." He pulled out a whip and began to strike her repeatedly.

Ann tried to ignore Ceara's cries of pain but felt a pang of sadness.

"Think about your mistakes. As much as I'd like to punish you more, I have other matters to take care of," Urien said, spitting at Ceara. "Constance, you know how to be obedient, don't you?" He caressed the face of a blond Gliss.

"Of course, my lord."

Ceara's eyes flashed. "Urien, you can't just cast me aside."

Urien grabbed Ceara by the throat, yanking her up. "*Never* tell me what I can and cannot do!" He squeezed until Ceara's eyes rolled back in her head, then threw her to the floor again.

"What about the body?" Constance asked, motioning to Ann.

"Leave it here and let Ceara learn her place."

The door banged as Urien and the other Gliss left the room.

"Ceara?" Ann hissed. She had no idea if the Gliss would be able to hear her or not. If she could convince her to pull the knife out, it might be enough to free herself. "Ceara, wake up! I thought a Gliss would be stronger than this. Urien's right, you are weak."

Ceara's eyes flashed as she turned toward Ann. "How dare you call me weak!" she rasped.

"I'll kill you."

"When are you people ever going to learn? *I can't die.*" Ann crossed her arms. "Urien turned on you just like I said he would."

Ceara wiped her face as a tear dripped down her cheek. "I'm not weak. I-I failed him. I didn't—"

"Oh, for spirits' sake, what kind of Gliss loses it over a man?" Ann demanded. "Gliss are supposed to be strong, ruthless bitches. Look at you, you're pathetic!"

"It's my duty to serve Orla and her son."

"Urien could care less about you. Instead of whining, why don't you get angry?" Ann said. "You've waited five years to have him back, and he's getting cosy with someone else already."

Ceara scrambled up. "If that bastard thinks he can treat me this way, he's wrong." She pulled the knife free, and Ann sat up. She muttered words of power, but Ceara grabbed her arm. "Wait, you can't use magic. Urien will sense it." She yanked Ann free from the circle. "Urien didn't become archdruid, did he?"

Ann shook her head. "No."

Ceara nodded. "Good. If you're going to stop Urien, I'll be there to help you."

CHAPTER 21

Ann couldn't believe her ears. She didn't doubt Ceara's need to get revenge, but that didn't mean she could trust the Gliss.

"Urien will know I'm alive the moment we walk out of this room if he doesn't know already," Ann said. "We need a plan." She swayed a little, still feeling weak from the blood loss.

"If I kill the guards, he won't know unless you use magic," Ceara said. "We'll find Urien and—"

"And do what? You can't kill him. Our father cast a spell to protect us from death–he did it to stop Urien from killing us."

Ceara arched a brow. "You don't look to be in any fit state to take him on either."

"I don't plan to. I need a way out of here."

Ceara snorted. "You'll never get out of the palace alive, and you can't leave while Urien occupies Xander's body. He has your aunt too."

"I—what? Damn Orla!" Ann ran a hand through her hair. "Urien must suspect I'm still alive. He'd know that ritual wouldn't have been enough to break the link. But why is he keeping you around?"

"To punish me. I say we strike now. Xander's body is still weak."

As am I, she thought. *I need time to recharge my energy too, but I doubt I'll get do that with an impatient Gliss around.*

"We need to be ready." Ann gripped the knife Urien had used on her, and Ceara pulled out one of her rods. "I've got to find my aunt, then I'm leaving."

"Urien has to die!"

"I'm not sure he *can* die, but I need to be at full strength if you want my help to defeat him."

"Defeat him?" Ceara snorted. "I want to crucify him!"

"You can't, at least not while he's in Xander's body. Xander's soul is still there, trapped by Urien's."

Ceara's fists clenched. "You yanked Urien's soul out of his body before, can't you do it again?"

"Urien didn't have Xander's powers then. He's even stronger now, but that doesn't mean I won't try." She wiped some of the dry blood off her arms. "Ready?"

"I was born ready." Ceara grinned and banged on the door. "Let me out of here!"

Ann gripped the knife, wishing she could summon magic.

"Hey!" Ceara yelled. "I shouldn't be stuck in here with a rotting corpse." She banged again. "I want to talk to Urien!"

The door creaked open. Ceara grabbed the Gliss on the other side, slicing the woman's throat before she had a chance to react. "Natasha always was a weakling," Ceara muttered, shoving the dead Gliss aside and bolting from the room.

As Ann followed her, three more appeared in the hallway. Ceara threw one of her knives at one, blocking a blow from another.

The third Gliss made a grab for Ann, who punched her in the face. The Gliss grabbed Ann by the throat, and she felt the burn of her magic being used against her. Thrusting her knife up, she stabbed the Gliss in the shoulder, pulled back, and smashed the Gliss' head against the wall.

Ceara grabbed the Gliss and slashed her throat. "We're supposed to kill them, not knock them out."

"I was about to! Forgive me if I don't have the killer instinct like you," Ann said.

Ceara ignored the remark and turned down the hall. "Let's go."

Ann leaned against the wall, taking a few deep breaths as she felt slivers of power seep back into her veins.

"Come on, Rhiannon. We don't have time to dawdle."

Ann frowned as she felt a familiar presence—Edward. He was somewhere near the palace. "Not yet." She grabbed Ceara's arm. "This way." She pulled the Gliss in the opposite direction.

"There's nothing down here!"

Ann felt along the wall until she found the part that opened. "Come on, this way."

"But Urien—"

Ann shoved Ceara through and closed the wall behind them.

"—is the other way," Ceara hissed.

"I told you, we need a plan of attack," Ann said. "These passages lead down to where the Black used to live. We should be safe there—unless Orla used it?"

"No, the Gliss headquarters are in the East Wing. The Black's quarters are closed off," Ceara replied.

"Good, let's move."

"But—" Ceara protested.

Ann sighed. "Barging in there and attacking Urien won't do any good. I need time to gather my strength. I'm sure you can wait a couple of hours."

Ceara gritted her teeth. "I want him to suffer!"

"He will, but we both need rest. You're injured too."

Ceara snorted and rubbed her back. "I'm fine. Gliss are taught to withstand pain."

"You still need to treat those wounds."

As they moved along, Ann found her way through the tunnels easily, surprised by how well she remembered them from sneaking through them with Ed as a child.

At the entrance, she pushed the wall open to find Ed and Jax standing on the other side.

Ed breathed a sigh of relief when he saw her. "Hey, are you okay?"

"No." She threw herself into his arms, resting her head against his shoulder.

"What happened?" Ed pulled her close, his hold comforting.

"Some things never change," Ceara remarked, rolling her eyes.

Ed pulled away, eyes burning amber. "What is she doing here?"

"It's alright, she helped me escape." Ann touched his arm. "She's on our side."

"You can't be serious. She's a Gliss," he growled.

Ann pulled away as she felt something jolt through him.

"Here we go again," said Jax. "He's losing control. Ann—"

She cupped Ed's face. "It's okay, Ceara isn't a threat."

"Right, I've no interest in killing anyone but Urien," said Ceara, gripping her rod. "I'm not here to hurt anyone."

"Forgive me if I don't take the word of a Gliss at face value," Jax said.

"Stand down, all of you," Ann ordered. "No one is hurting anyone. Put your weapons down." She glanced at Ed, and his eyes returned to normal.

"Why is she here?" he hissed.

"Because she can help. Urien is inside Xander's body," Ann explained.

Edward's eyes widened. "How?"

"Orla used my blood to bring him back."

"Bastard!" Ceara muttered. "If he thinks he can treat me like a—"

Sage appeared, pushing past the two men to get to Ann. "Have you seen Flora?"

"No, but she's here somewhere. We need a plan."

Ann splashed cold water on her face, trying to wash away some of the blood while Sage and the others argued over the best course of action to take. Ceara wanted to barge in and strike Urien head-on, but the others all agreed that would be the worst thing to do.

"How are you feeling?" Sage said as she came over to sit beside her.

"My murderous half-brother has come back and now resides inside my good brother, how do you think I feel?" Ann ran a hand through her hair and sighed. "I don't know if can face him again. I only stopped him last time because of my pain at what he did."

"You're strong. You helped people with magic escape from Orla's clutches for years, but now is the time to start embracing your true power."

"What are you talking about?" Ann frowned.

"You know Darius' power never went to Urien. You've always had the power of the archdruid, and you're the strongest one of us left."

She shook her head. "Papa's power never went anywhere, and even if it did, the power of an archdruid doesn't make me one," she said. "I'm not my father."

"Darius is gone, and yet here you are. You need to remember who you are, Rhiannon."

"I'm not…" She protested again and stopped. Deep down she'd always known she changed that night. She'd stopped being Rhiannon Valeran, the Druid's daughter. And she'd become someone else.

"No, you're stronger than him. Strength doesn't come from a spell, but within." Sage patted her hand. "Why else do you think Edward and Jax follow you?"

"Ed has always been with me, and…" She shook her head and rose. "Enough!" she snapped at the others. "We are wasting time here. It's time my brother and I had a little chat."

Ann pushed open the heavy doors to the great hall. It felt odd being back here, the days of it being home felt like a distant memory now.

Urien sat on the archdruid's throne, smiling as she walked in. "Sister, how nice of you to join us."

She spotted Flo in the corner, surrounded by Gliss but seemingly unharmed.

"Hello, brother." Ann strode toward him. "Let's cut the chitchat since I doubt we have much to talk about."

"Of course we do. You're still my sister." He motioned to the empty throne beside him. "Please sit. Your place is by my side."

Her eyes widened, but she hid her surprise as she marched up the steps and onto the dais, before slumping onto her throne. "Now what?" she asked. "You start reorganising Caselhelm? Because I won't be part of that."

"Come now, Rhiannon. I know we've had our differences, but I don't see why we can't work together."

"*Differences?* You murdered my parents, and now you're inside Xander's body." Ann crossed her arms.

Urien's smile widened. "If you'd tell me where my own body is, I wouldn't have to be."

"Even if I knew, I wouldn't tell you." She stared at him. "Xander's still inside you, isn't he? I'd know if he were gone." She scanned him with her mind, but the cold, icy feel of Urien's energy made it impossible for her to find any trace of Xander.

"Perhaps, but never mind him. I don't want to kill you," Urien said and rose. "We're family. We should rule together. We'll be unstoppable." He walked down the steps and made a move toward her.

Ann stepped back. It felt strange enough seeing Xander's body move and act like Urien. She did not want him touching her. "What makes you think I'd join you after everything you've done?" Her eyes narrowed. "Everything you've put me through? You killed my parents, why would I trust you?"

"Remember when you were little, and I used to bring you gifts?" Urien smiled. "We were close once."

She winced, remembering how kind he'd been to her. Despite being two years older than her, he'd always been kind to her as a child. "That was a long time ago. We've both changed."

She glanced over at Flo. *Are you alright?*

Flo gave a slight nod but said nothing.

"Yes, you've become a rogue druid helping outcasts and freaks. I saw more than you think on the other side. Our father deserved death, especially after he cast me into that hell realm. He didn't deserve to sit here, either. For all the lands to be united, they need someone strong and powerful to lead them. He was weak, pathetic." Urien sneered and clenched his hands into fists.

Ann tried to hide her surprise. He thought Darius had banished him when he'd cast the binding spell before he died? Maybe she could use that to her advantage.

"What makes you think the people would ever follow you?" Ann asked.

"I'm the archdruid. I'm stronger than our father. As his heir, it's my right to rule," he said. "The five lands have been in chaos for centuries. Entire races are enslaved or at risk of going extinct. Father might have given them the illusion of order, but I'll give them true freedom. Peace. The likes of which the lands have never known."

He is more delusional than I imagined.

"Think about it, Ann," Urien said in Xander's voice. "We can be a family again. Isn't that what you want? To belong? To feel part of something again?"

Now he's trying to play on my emotions. She shook her head. "I have a family, people who will stick by me no matter what. You will never be part of that."

Taking her cue, Ceara moved out of the shadows and threw a knife at him.

Urien dodged it, staring down at the blade that had embedded itself in his chair. "What is this?" he demanded and glowered at Ceara. "You stupid bitch, you know I can't die. I'm immortal now."

"Immortal? Ha! Papa cast a spell on us before he died. No doubt to stop us from killing each other," Ann snapped.

All of the Gliss moved forward, and one of them grabbed Flo.

Jax and Ed burst into the room and started attacking them. Ed shifted into his beast form, his emerald eyes blazing as he grabbed hold of the first Gliss that came at him.

"No one casts me aside," Ceara snarled. She pulled out one of her rods, lunging at Urien. He dodged her and struck her with a bolt of lightning. Ceara hit the floor, grunting with pain.

Ann raised her hand, sending a column of fire surging straight toward her brother.

Ed, get Flo and get her out of here!

I'm trying!

Urien dodged the flames. "You're turning against me, just like Father did." He glared at her.

"You're not the archdruid, and I can't have you harming anyone else." More fire shot from her hands. Urien tried to fight back, but Ceara grabbed him and held him down.

"Ceangail agus díbirt a anam." Ann recited the spell, just as she had the night she banished him all those years ago. She raised her hand and reached for his spirit, only to feel a shield there.

Urien laughed, shoving Ceara aside. "Not this time, sister. I won't go back to that hell, and you can't stop me without harming Xander too."

Lightning flew out of his hand.

Ann deflected it with another burst of flames but stumbled backwards. Energy shot around the room, causing explosions in its wake, and she and Urien struggled as their magic clashed against each other.

She raised her hand again, power flaring between her fingers in fiery hit sparks. She couldn't let Urien get away. Ann had to say the spell one more time and attempt to remove Urien's soul.

Urien shot to his feet and grabbed hold of Flora. "You won't stop me this time, Rhiannon. I'm more powerful than I've ever been," he snarled. "It'll take more than your power to remove me from

Xander's body." He smiled at Flo. "Aunt Flora, you were always kind

to me growing up. Unlike my bastard father." He ran a finger over

her cheek. "Always did have a soft heart, didn't you? There can be no

room for weakness under my rule." Lightning flared between his

fingers.

"No!" Ed yelled. Flora's eyes widened in shock as static jolted

through her and she slumped to the floor.

Ed caught hold of her as Urien backed away, laughing as he and

his Gliss surrounded them.

Ceara gasped, staring at them in disbelief.

Ann rushed over, along with Jax, who used his stone ability to

harden his skin and pummel a couple of Gliss out of the way.

"Mum?" Jax said.

Ann met Ed's eyes and her heart twisted as he shook his head. Flo

was gone.

"One way or another, brother, I will find a way to stop you." She

sent Urien crashing across the room. Grabbing hold of Ed and Jax's

arms, she spoke the spell for transference, and the four of them

disappeared in a flash of light.

They buried Flora on Trin, gathering together at the top of the tor to say their final goodbyes. Ann felt numb as she said an invocation to the spirits and Jax and Ed carried Flo's body down into the underground tombs beneath the tor. Archdruids had been buried on the island for centuries, so it was a fitting place to bury her among the ancestors. Sage seemed to have aged after what happened.

"Urien won't stop," she told Ann after the service. "He'll plunge the lands into even more chaos than his mother did. Now he has Xander's power…" Her voice trailed off as she stared out of the water into the distance.

"And I'll be there to thwart his every attempt," Ann said. "The time for hiding is over. Now is the time to fight back."

If you enjoyed this book please leave a review on Amazon or book site of your choice.

***

For updates on more books and news releases sign up for my newsletter on tiffanyshand.com/newsletter

ALSO BY TIFFANY SHAND

The Shifter Clans Complete Box Set

TALES OF THE ITHEREAL

Fey Spy

Outcast Fey

Rogue Fey

Hunted Fey

Tales of the Ithereal Complete Box Set

THE FEY GUARDIAN SERIES

Memories Lost

Memories Awakened

Memories Found

The Fey Guardian Complete Series

THE ARKADIA SAGA

Chosen Avatar

Captive Avatar

Fallen Avatar

The Arkadia Saga Complete Series

ABOUT THE AUTHOR

Tiffany Shand is a writing mentor, professionally trained copy editor and copy writer who has been writing stories for as long as she can remember. Born in East Anglia, Tiffany still lives in the area, constantly guarding her workspace from the two cats which she shares her home with.

She began using her pets as a writing inspiration when she was a child, before moving on to write her first novel after successful completion of a creative writing course. Nowadays, Tiffany writes urban fantasy and paranormal romance, as well as nonfiction books for other writers, all available through eBook stores and on her own website.

Tiffany's favourite quote is *'writing is an exploration. You start from nothing and learn as you go'* and it is armed with this that she hopes to be able to help, inspire and mentor many more aspiring authors.

When she has time to unwind, Tiffany enjoys photography, reading, and watching endless box sets. She also loves to get out and visit the vast number of castles and historic houses that England has to offer.

You can contact Tiffany Shand, or just see what she is writing about at:

Author website: tiffanyshand.com

Business site: Write Now Creative

Twitter: @tiffanyshand

Facebook page: Tiffany Shand Author Page

Printed in Poland
by Amazon Fulfillment
Poland Sp. z o.o., Wrocław
22 June 2022

10b1d8c6-5e34-42bc-ace0-9d7754a867b4R01